Indentical Strangers
Cleve Bush

☲ WINN PUBLICATIONS

For information address Winn Publications, 90 Coporate Park Drive Suite C703, Irvine, CA 92606.

Library of Congress Control Number: 2020919012

ISBN: 978-1-7349507-4-8

Indentical Strangers
Cleve Bush

Winn Publications LLC
Abilene, TX

Dedication

I would like to dedicate my debut novel, *Identical Strangers,* to Malik A. Rafsanjani, without your mentorship and guidance, this work would not be possible. Although life ended due to unforeseen circumstances, the legacy lives on.

To all the women of color who have sacrificed and surpassed all boundaries and obstacles placed before them, my love, life, and loyalty is forever imparted.

Unnatural Conception

I am the ultimate result of psychotic conception

But wait it gets worse

Separated from my twin at birth

Will prove be both a gift and a curse

Uncle Sam constantly and consistently screwed me

Ejaculating his seeds of hate

Injecting his DNA brutally

My entire environment—beautiful

But wreaking havoc mutually…

By the time trouble rotates 360degrees

Satan will have wished he expelled his seeds in the gutter

The female prisoners of war that you raped

Each metaphorically my mother

These unnatural acts of torture that you unleashed

That you'll witness—the ones that it'll

hurt to see—are called

A fair exchange for all

The lives that were claimed

The queens who birthed me

I'm lost, tormented—torn to pieces spiritually

A sister of the struggle since the beginning

Life's hell on Earth, literally

Androgynous, both masculine and feminine, physically,

A sight to behold, a gem of gold, eye candy, visually

If the price is right I contract your life

I'm the reaper times infinity

Table of Contents

CHAPTER 1

The brutal screams that pierced the hollow emptiness of the Somalian jungle could be heard for miles, alarming even the most undaunted citizens. Be that as it may, the inhabitants, at best, could only assume that this was just another identification echo—referred to as the call of the wild.

The thick brush of the forest surrounded them, concealing the atrocities of war. There was no way out for Destiny, her only escape were the gut wrenching screams and yells that she hoped would bring her rescue.

Her soul and body were encountering the ultimate violation, a one-dimensional act to which she could give no reciprocation. She had signed up for the love of her country, but her country had not reciprocated that love. They had abandoned her and allowed her to be captured. They had turned the other cheek, and now these savages were ravaging her body. At this point, she had lost track of how many times the stench of the men upon her body had invaded her sense of smell. Their scent reeked of evil.

Was this the third or the fourth time? She really couldn't be sure, but she was resigned. Finally, as the last hollow scream escaped her body, she accepted her situation. She realized she had to cooperate. It was her only hope of getting home alive. The violent acts that the Somalian rebels were committing against her were a direct response to a deep-seated hate and disdain for Americans—especially African Americans.

Darkness had fallen upon her. Her body was so ravaged that she could no longer muster the strength to endure the torture. She was not sure how long she had been unconscious this time, or when they had decided to give her withered body respite.

In the distance, the sound of their evil voices began to rouse her. Before she knew it, the hungry whites of their eyes were upon her again. Her captors had returned. Destiny recognized the famished look of lust etched upon their countenance.

She could clearly gauge that the two men were communicating in different tongues. *How did they understand one another?* But then, she told herself that the language of violence was universal. Mentally preparing her escape, she closed her eyes, took a deep breath, and focused.

"You can do this," she whispered to herself as the imagery entered her mind of her very soul being forced to rise outside of her body. They were going to violate her, and there was nothing she could do about it. If this was going to happen, then she was not going to be there to endure it. The only way she could escape was mentally.

The pain of the chains binding her arms and legs imprisoned her, spread-eagle to cemented spikes in the ground. Before she knew it, the wretched stench of one of the rebels was piercing her body again. "Focus, Destiny", she told herself as the tears streamed down her face onto the cold cement. She lay helpless and lifeless.

She moaned as the pain continued to pierce her soul; unfortunately, the vile creature upon her mistook her pain for appreciation. She felt disgusted, humiliated, and powerless as she trembled to her core. He continued unleashing his rage upon her, as she felt she would vomit from his foul odor. The torture intensified into a loud crescendo of panting, until he finally collapsed upon her limp body and howled something in his native language, disgusting Destiny to her core. She lay both motionless and emotionless. Only her physical presence was there. The Rebel slowly removed himself from her body with a smirk of satisfaction. Little did he know that the brief moment of power he had only just enjoyed would prove to be his worst nightmare.

He slowly walked over to the nearby stream to collect a drink, while simultaneously gesturing the other rebel to cease torture of their prisoner. He had claimed possession of Destiny. For a moment, the other rebel appeared that he would defy his orders as testosterone flared between them. However, of the two, Destiny's most recent violator was the most evil, and his companion dared not cross him.

Infused with power and evil, he feigned a false sense of humanity, slowly freeing Destiny's arms to offer her a cool drink of water. Someone should have warned him that in war, a thirst for power over others was the number one killer of men.

Hours had passed, and her anger only intensified as she endured her captor enjoying the satisfaction of the power he had over her. However, his only mistake was not knowing how resourceful she was. He had no idea that she had planned far ahead if she were to encounter his kind of evil. She had passed out several times during the assault, but she never forgot the D-2 steel stiletto that she had covertly placed in the bun of her hair.

Thankfully, he had allowed her hands to remain free. She was not bound, and as he slowly approached her, she calculated her next move.

He looked her directly in the eyes with a scrowl that caue her insides to boil while attempting to return her to the restraints of bondage. As he slowly kneeled, Destiny attacked with the agility of a lioness on the hunt. With all the force she could muster, she wedged the weapon at a perfect angle through the larynx of her tormentor and then deep into the meninges of his brain. She knew immediately that he was dead. It happened so quickly that he did not have time to warn his companions .

Swiftly, she took her escape. Gasping for air and ignoring the pain that haunted her body from the ordeal she had only just endured, she navigated her way through the thick of the wilderness with only a compass that she had confiscated from her captors.

As rage and panic overtook her at once, Destiny clutched the shadows of the wilderness, retracing her steps desperately to find the company from which she had been separated. Finally, as the thick of wilderness began to clear, she could see it in the far distance—the six seat Z-Boat.

Pain invaded her entire being, but she couldn't give up; she had to make it! "Run for it," she whispered, as she pushed herself into a full sprint. Before she knew it, Destiny had come face to face with the members of her SEAL team through hazy eyes. She had made it back alive. She couldn't believe it. They all stared in shock as she eerily began to recant the Navy SEAL Philosophy:

"I will never quit … My nation expects me to be physically harder and mentally stronger than my enemies. If knocked down, I will get back up every time. I will draw on every remaining ounce of strength to protect my teammates … I am never out of the fight."

Darkness fell upon Destiny again.

CHAPTER 2

Gazing out of the aircraft carrier, all Destiny could do was shield her eyes as they floated upon the docks of 32nd Street Naval Station in San Diego, California. It had been weeks since her ordeal, and now she was returning to the states where she felt safe. However, more importantly, it would be where she would begin to reclaim her life. She dreaded exiting the carrier as it felt as if all eyes were fixed on her. "Are you ready?" the gruff but comforting voice asked her as he softly caressed her shoulder.

He was her longtime mentor and confidante, Master Chief Cox. She truly felt that she would not have made it through the past few weeks without him. Unlike anyone else in her life, he had encouraged her to stay strong and reassured her that she was just as strong and resilient as any of the male SEALs and that she would survive.

"It's now or never," Destiny replied with a sigh as they exited the aircraft.

Suddenly, it seemed as if the world were moving at an accelerated pace. With Cox at her side holding her hand the entire way, she furiously pushed and shoved her way through the cluttered deck. She couldn't bear to think of making eye contact with anyone.

Did they know what I had gone through in Somalia? The thought alone and the sheer humiliation that accompanied it caused her to shutter. As they continued to soar through the crowd, Destiny could not force herself to walk past the flag. Although she felt a deep seeded disappointment in what her own country had allowed to happen to her, she finally raised her head and slowed her pace just long enough to salute. After everything, it still represented something real to her. It was in some strange way the reason she had survived.

They finally reached an area where the crowd cleared and there it was—the van that was awaiting their arrival. Keeping in perfect step with Cox, she raced full speed to the awaiting van. *Finally, I can breathe,* she thought to herself as she collapsed in the passenger van.

"Are you okay?" Cox asked as if concerned. "I'm fine," Destiny replied with a sense of insecurity. "Don't worry," replied Cox. "Once we get to the personnel building, you will be fine." A thick cloud of silence drifted between them for the remainder of the ride as Destiny gazed out of the window of the moving van.

"I have to be strong," she repeatedly affirmed to herself. "I have to be strong." The personnel building, unfortunately, was buzzing with just as many people as she had encountered getting off the aircraft carrier. She was grateful to have Cox at her side as they approached the yeoman's desk. "You must be Ms. Destiny Dupree," the woman inquired. Although the woman knew nothing of Destiny's ordeal, from Destiny's perspective, she was eyeing her with a sense of pity, and for that, Destiny was resentful. Cox immediately sensed Destiny's discomfort.

"She knows nothing," he quietly whispered in Destiny's ear. "No one does." Destiny took a sigh of relief and she reached for the leave papers along with her pay. "So, where do we go from here?" she asked Cox. "Well, I know you've had a lot of care, but we want you to be examined again here."

Destiny's mind wandered back to her encounter at the naval hospital in Africa. The sexual assault nurse had been very kind to her, but she couldn't imagine having to go through all of that again. "Why do I need care now?" she asked. "It's over, Cox! It happened, and I need to move on!" "Destiny, you have been through a terrible ordeal. The level of care that you have received over the past few weeks is nothing compared to what you will get here in the States. Now, you will see another nurse at the Balboa Naval Hospital, and don't argue with me. We just want to make sure that you are going to be okay. After this, we'll get to work on moving forward. Deal?" Destiny could sense the sincerity in Cox's demands. She knew she was blessed to have such a loyal and dedicated mentor. "Okay," she reluctantly agreed with an air of exasperation. "I'll do it, but this is the last time. I'm not a victim, you know. I refuse to be a victim … I'm a damn SEAL, Cox … a goddam SEAL!"

The drive to the hospital was just as nerve wrecking as the entire day had been. She was immediately greeted by yet another S.A.N.E. (Sexual Assault Nurse Examiner), and put through yet another battery of exams. "You are welcome to get dressed now," the nurse softly said as she exited the room.

Unresponsive, Destiny stared at white pristine walls of the examination room. *Why am I being put through this all over again*, she thought to herself. "Ms. Dupree, did you hear me?" the nurse asked. Suddenly jarred from her stupor, Destiny replied. "I'm sorry, what did you say?" Destiny asked. "I said you can get dressed now. Just make yourself comfortable. I'll be back in a few minutes with the results of your tests."

Just as she started to exit the examination room, the nurse paused and made a sudden sharp turn toward Destiny. "Ms. Dupree," she said as she made direct eye contact with Destiny. "I don't know your story, but I know it's going to be okay." Destiny didn't respond. She only stared at the woman as the tears flooded her eyes, and with the clicking sound of the door, she collapsed her tear-filled face onto her hands.

###

"Pregnant?" Destiny panicked with question. "That can't be right! I mean, there must be some kind of mistake. I …I can't be." "I'm sorry, Ms. Dupree, but the test is highly accurate. Yes, you are pregnant. We ran the test several times to be sure," the nurse replied. "We will make sure you have all the resources you need and are aware of all your options…" "Options?" Destiny angrily interjected. "Cox, this can't be happening to me. Please, tell me this is not happening." As usual, Cox was right at her side consoling her, holding her hand. "I'm sorry Destiny, but don't throw yourself into a fullblown panic attack. We can fix this. You will be okay."

Learning she was with child only added more devastation to the chain of events that she had recently endured. "What do you mean we will fix it?" she asked Cox. "Well … I … I," Cox stuttered. "I'm sure you don't want to go through with this pregnancy… Do you? "I can't kill a child," Destiny desperately whispered. "I just can't!"

After four months of refusing to abort, Destiny began to develop a close bond to the life that was materializing inside of her womb. Her greatest disappointment was Cox. Despite exercising her right to keep her child, he, along with her other senior leaders, truly believed that the trauma she endured in Somalia had driven her mad. After learning of the pregnancy, she had been forced to endure a full and extensive psychiatric evaluation. To add insult to injury, her leave had been revoked, and she was placed on light duty, consisting of rest, counseling, and six months of psychiatric tests and evaluations.

However, Destiny had remained strong. As usual, she awoke daily at 0400 for her morning workout routine, and although she was increasing in size and well ahead of the predicted weight that the physician had suggested, today would be no different. The sound of the alarm was a welcome interruption of her restless night. The nightmares were unbearable at times. Many nights, she found herself back in the Somalian jungle, only to abruptly awake drenched in her own sweat.

Groggily, she reached over to the bedside table, and with a single gesture, the alarm ceased, only to be followed by a very familiar ring tone. It was Cox. "Good morning , Cox." She greeted him with an air of cynicism. "Good morning, Destiny," Cox retorted. "I know it's early, but I thought I would check on you before you headed to the gym. Are you sure you should be working out so vigorously?" "Yes, I'm sure Cox," she replied. "Don't worry about me. I was cleared by the physician to continue my normal workout routine. He actually agrees with me and says it good for me and the baby. I don't want you to worry. I promise, if I develop any issues I will pull back, but I need normalcy in my life. Keeping my routine really helps. So don't worry. I'll be fine."

Cox took a deep breath. He was truly worried about Destiny, no matter how adamant she was about being fine. He knew better than anyone else that she was not fine. He knew the truth, and he knew far more than Destiny knew herself. "Well, I'll layoff," Cox relented, "but don't forget about our appointment today. I'll meet you at the physician's office at 1100." "You don't have to do that," Destiny demanded. "I'm a big girl, Cox. I can handle this."

Dead silence emanated from the opposite line. "Cox… Are you still there?" "Yea … Yea … um, I want to be a part of this Destiny. I'll be with you until the end—the very end. See you later today."

Still unable to shake the nightmares that had kept her awake on the previous night, Destiny struggled with focusing on her normal workout routine. Usually she would have headed directly to the treadmill after stretching, but not today, she needed to clear her head. So, her normal stretching was followed by a deep dive in the Olympic-sized pool. She remained under the heated waters for three minutes before she finally surfaced. Unfortunately, she was still unable to focus, yet still determined to clear her head. She consider the treadmill again for a second, but before she knew it, she had taken off on her six mile run.

After only a mile into her run, she was drenched. The more she was haunted by the dreams, the harder she ran—and the more she became drenched with sweat. She often questioned why she worked so hard, but the sweat emanating from her pores had become a metaphorical symbol that she was cleansing herself of the toxins that her attackers had poisoned her body with.

Unfortunately, the confusion between the bond that she felt to the life growing inside her and the deep-seated hate that she felt for evil responsible for that life, ravaged at her mind every second of the day. The beeping of the timer told her that she was on her last lap. Fortunately, the run had worked. As her mind had slowed, she too slowed down to a fast paced walk. At the end of the lap, she settled on the bench, eyeing the bump on her abdomen that seemed to have appeared overnight. She didn't know much about having babies, but she knew for sure that she was growing pretty fast.

"Hello, little one," she whispered as she caressed her stomach. "I'll get to meet you today, and don't worry. We'll be okay. Mama's going to make sure of that."

As a tear escaped the corner of her eye, Destiny slowly lifted herself from the bench. She realized that she still had time to swing by the local bookstore. She wanted to give her child a bold and strong name, and a few books might just help her with that.

She felt that no one would truly comprehend her commitment to bringing her child into the world, regardless of how he or she was conceived. However, the child was all she had. Having been an only child and losing both her mother and father at a young age, she had no remaining family. The thought of having a child gave her a sense of belonging and she felt a sense of pride that one day, she would have the opportunity to leave a piece of herself behind—her own legacy.

Despite the violent nature in which her child was conceived, Destiny could sense that the baby in which she was carrying had all the ingredients of greatness. While she hated her assailants, she knew her baby carried in its veins the pure blood of Mother Africa, and combined with the will-power and determination of the first African American Female Navy SEAL, this child could not lose.

As the ultra sonographer applied the cool gel to her abdomen, Destiny nervously squeezed Cox's hand as he stood at her side. The rolling of her device over the small hill that was forming in her midsection caused her to quiver a bit, but with Cox there she knew she would be fine. "Are you okay?" the sonographer asked. "Yes," Destiny replied. "Just a little nervous." "Well, I have a good view," she replied. "Would you like to see?"

Destiny traded glances with Cox for reassurance as he gave her nod. "Yes," she whispered. "Is the baby healthy?" "Well," the sonographer replied. "Take a look at this screen. All the fingers and toes are there, but we have bit of a surprise."

"Surprise?" Destiny nervously questioned as she wearily eyed the screen of the ultrasound machine. "Is there a problem?" "I'm not sure," the sonographer replied. "It depends on you. If you look on this side of your abdomen, there is a little one with ten fingers antd ten toes."

However, she continued as she applied more of the cold gel and navigated to the other side of Destiny's abdomen. "Here we have another little with all its fingers and toes … and listen to this."

The soothing sound of double heartbeats invaded the room. Destiny was in shock by the pulsating sound, she did not say a word. "Are they healthy?" Cox asked. "Absolutely," replied the sonographer as she exited the room, "—as far as I can see, but the doctor will be able to tell you more. Otherwise, it appears you have two healthy baby girls, Ms. Dupree."

Destiny was jarred out of her stupor by the announcement that the babies were girls. *Wow, this is so overwhelming,* she thought to herself— *twin girls?* "Yes," the Physician said as he suddenly entered the room. "Ms. Dupree, it looks like you are carrying twins."

CHAPTER 3

Over seven months and passed since Destiny's return from hell. As she exited the Navy Hospital, she took a sigh of relief. She had been released from her light duty with a favorable evaluation from her psychiatrist. Other than the two occupants in her body, that were growing daily, Destiny had formed many bonds as she journeyed through the healing process. Admittedly, the physicians learned a great deal about humanity from her and greatly admired her bravery.

She felt far more clear and focused than she had in months as she headed out of the parking lot. Taking notice of the signs that lead to the San Diego Zoo, she laughed to herself about her quirky fondness of reptiles, especially snakes. Many people found her fondness of snakes to be quite funny. However, someday it would not be so funny at all.

Packing the last of her bags, Destiny couldn't wait to get to her destination. She had decided to take a thirty day sabbatical, which was agreed upon by both she and her psychiatrist. As the highway morphed into Interstate 8, she let the summer wind blow through her hair as the poetic melody of Erykah Badu's singing eased her mind. Driving in the desert only added to her sense of calm. She had spent a lot of time out there studying mephitic species of snakes and scorpions that exist in the region. She was more than aware that researching alone was not always safe. Unlike the zoo, there were no safety nets when in the desert alone, and the reptiles that she adored so much could be very deadly if their natural habitat was disturbed. However, as she crossed the border into Yuma, Arizona, she felt the rumble of butterflies in the pit of her stomach.

Finally, something she was drawn to, through both the fascination of it and the danger. Pulling into the campground, she cut the ignition off and pulled her Bible out. There were many things about herself that she kept sacred. Although she was far from a religious fanatic and adhered to no particular faith, she had a spiritual side that she shared with no one—not even Cox. Most of all, she deeply believed her Scorpio zodiac sign bonded her to these dangerous reptiles that she felt so deeply connected to.

One thing her ordeal in captivity had taught her was to live her life, and she promised herself that she would live as if each day were her last. She was a realist, and she fully understood the push and pull of powers and principalities. Turning to the scriptures, Destiny said a quick prayer and began to read Psalm 23:2 :

He maketh me to lie down in green pastures.
He leadeth me beside still waters; He restoreth my soul. He leadeth me in the path of righteousness for his names sake. Yea, though I walk through the valley of the shadow of death I will fear no evil, for thou art with me, thy rod and thy staff, they comfort me. Thou preparest a table before me In the presence of mine enemies, Thou anointest my head with oil; My cup runneth over. Surely goodness and mercy shall follow me all the days of my life. And I will dwell in the house of the Lord forever. Amen.

Destiny raised her head from the Bible and blew a kiss at the large bump that had overtaken her midsection. "Are you guys ready?" she asked. "Let's go meet your family."

###

It wasn't long before the sweltering sun began to dissipate. She realized that she had spent enough time in the desert, and had not had much luck in coming across many of her reptilian friends. However, a cloud was brewing overhead, and it was time to move on. Just as she had suspected, the terrain en route to San Diego was a dangerous drive ranging hundreds of feet above sea level to hundreds below and wrapping around the mountains along the way. The limited visibility, reckless commercial vehicles, and drivers on cell phones in two-way traffic did not help at all. Destiny knew she needed to be extra cautious. She had accepted that she was responsible for more than just her own life now, and the conditions that she was driving in was a recipe for an accident waiting to happen.

The eerie screech of the windshield wipers, along with the animated light shining brilliantly in the rear view mirror caused Destiny to ride the brakes as she passed the road sign warning of 200 ft above sea level. As she descended the spiraling mountain, she was startled by the sound of a horn from a passing truck, forcing her to grip the steering wheel even tighter. Lately, life has become one big ball of fear. For in the past, she had never been startled so easily. Fear seemed to follow her everywhere she went. Fear that every black man was a rapist; fear that every snake and scorpion she encountered would strike at any moment; fear of raising her baby girls as bastards; fear of being on the highway. Ultimately, Destiny's fear equated to nothing less than a fear of death.

The deafening blare of the horn, the grinding of metal, and sudden bursts of whooshing air pockets warned her of an impending doom as she braced herself for the impact. Swerving to the east, an 18 wheeler monster clipped the left side of her bumper, plunging the car head first into the brown of the mountainside. As the car plummeted down, Destiny let out a blood curdling scream. "I don't want to die!" She desperately called out.

Suddenly, she felt an impact as her head slammed into the steering column and darkness fell upon her.

The scene was gruesome. The entire interstate was closed off for hours. Unfortunately, Destiny was completely unrecognizable. The only ways to identify the beautiful young woman was through her military I.D badges. Once notified, Cox rushed to the scene maneuvering around the police and emergency technicians. He personally unfastened the seat belt as he wept over her broken body. "I can't believe you're gone," Cox whispered as he suddenly took notice of her bulging abdomen. "The twins!" Cox yelled out. "She's pregnant with twins—we have to save them!"

Destiny's clothes were soaked with blood. It was impossible to tell where the blood was coming from, and Cox dreaded that the twins were gone too. Seconds later, the chopper landed, and within minutes, the EMTs were frantically fighting to save the lives of the twins. "We're going to have to remove the babies now, or they won't stand a chance!" the medic yelled out.

The world had lost a strong and beautiful young woman, but for her sacrifice, the world would now have two more. The medics carefully removed the twins from Destiny's womb. However, at seven months gestation, their chances of being able to breathe on their own were highly questionable. "They may need surfactant to breathe," the medic yelled out. "We have to get them to the hospital."

Soon, the chopper was descending upon Balboa Hospital. As the doors flung open into the sterility of the emergency room, the medical team, already on alert, went to work to save the lives of the children.

Cox had sat in the waiting room for twelve hours before the doctor came out. "We've done all we can do," he calmly informed Cox. "The rest is up to the girls."

Cox didn't flinch, but coldly stared at the wall. He was overwhelmed with both shock and grief. *How could this have happened. Destiny was really gone.* "If they are anything like their mother," Cox suddenly spoke, "they will be just fine."

Although several weeks premature, the twins were healthy, thriving and growing with each passing day. However, baby girls Dupree one and two had yet to be named. Destiny's pediatric physician and Cox, her chief commander, stood just outside the hospital nursery awaiting the meeting that would decide the names of the Dupree babies. "Chief Officer Cox, I presume?" The physician asked. "Yes," Cox replied, as he turned to face the two medical officers. "I am Doctor Wesley Mason, and this is Destiny's Psychiatris …" "Yes," Cox interrupted. "I am very familiar with Dr. Dandridge. Nice to see you again Dr. Dandridge. I just hate it's under such sad circumstances." "Yes," Dr. Dandridge agreed. " I feel the same way." "Well," Dr. Mason continued, "In respect of the legalities surrounding Ms. Dupree's case, you were contacted, Mr. Cox, because Destiny listed you as someone who could have direct access to her medical records. I contacted Dr. Dandridge to inform him of Destiny's untimely death, and that is when he informed me that her records contained information related to the naming of the children. While we can legally name the children, your signature will be required in lieu of Ms. Dupree's." "I understand," Cox replied. "Please follow me." Dr. Mason said as he gestured the other men into a conference room just off of the nursery. "I have here for you specifics in these files from Ms. Dupree pertaining to the naming of the girls." Dr. Dandridge explained. "As you can see here, Mr. Cox, this entry in Destiny's file is dated May 13th. Ironically, this was her last scheduled evaluation with me. Do you wish me to do the honors?" Cox nodded in agreement, and Dr. Dandridge began to read.

On this day , I have chosen the names of Fatimah and Khadijah for my daughters. After much thought, although I am of no particular faith, I am resigned to choosing these which are normally reserved for those who practice the Islamic faith. Based on the horrific manner in which my children were conceived, it is my hope that under the conditions in which my children were conceived that their names, in some manner, serve as a true symbol of the Islamic faith. I do not attribute terrorism and wickedness to this faith as many do.

Individual people can be wicked and vile—not an entire religious faith. As many do not understand me and who I am, they also do not understand my level of patriotism. However, it is my hope that by accepting my girls, you will embrace the true meaning of Islam. Peace is the accurate meaning, so please embrace peace, as this is what I offer my beautiful babies. In my own way, this is what I offer to the world through the introduction of Fatimah and Khadijah. Other than their names, my only request should something unexpected happen is that the smallest of the two be named Fatimah. This concludes my evaluation.

Thank you,
Ms. Destiny Dupree

Who Am I?

I am blasphemy, but don't get mad at me, a wasted sprout
of African erection
I am flesh of her flesh, the resurrection of Destiny
The inverse of passionate affection
I've been a menace since my entrance
Rape and torture made me
The descendant of original immigrants
I am the hate you gave me
I am the tide of the Nile
I am the shadows of the moon
With the instincts of the wild
Containing the energy of the sun
At the hottest hour of noon
Who am I
I am the daughter of the spirit
The Trifecta of the trinity
I am the music and the lyric
The song of stolen virginity
I am the candle in the dark
Awaiting the flame of eternal fire
I am the match and the spark
Giving light to nocturnal desire
I am the machination of imagination
The end result of affliction
I am the misfit for you to witness
Embalmed with holy spirit of perdition

CHAPTER 4

The Arlington National Cemetery seemed dreary and desolate as the funeral services for Petty Officer Destiny Dupree was being conducted. As the patriotic "Taps" was being performed, the eerie feel of souls rising from graves like vapor hung low in the air. The humongous flag flying at half-mast indicated to the state of Virginia that Uncle Sam was burying another child. Not only did Petty Officer Dupree hold the title of first female Navy SEAL, she was now being honored as the first female to receive the prestigious Purple Heart, the highest Medal of Honor; that can only be awarded posthumously.

Restricted to the care of medical personnel, Fatimah and Khadijah, along with the caseworker assigned by the State of California, stepped up to receive the military pittance of dog tags, a huge neatly folded flag, and a black lacquered case containing the Purple Heart. On cue, and as if possessed by the spiritual essence of all the soldiers' altruistic souls who lost their lives in the line of duty, the twins began to scream their indignant cries that brought a hush over the spectators as if they had just received a nefarious omen.

Concluding with the twenty-one gun salute, the trance that held the crowd temporarily hypnotized was broken, and the soldiers in unison conducted, left flank and saluted the American symbol of excellence as cannons roared through the air.

Sounds of the knolls gave validity to Destiny's demise. The lowering of the sarcophagus was the final act, indicating that this loss of life just broke the barriers of infinity. Encasing her jovial and intrepid spirit underneath piles of earth created an inverse effect and offset the world for years to come with the curse of her twins debauchery. The keystone being the benediction rendered by the Commander In Chief of the Armed Forces. Having placed his life in her hands a time or two during the course of his tenure, and also sharing in the elation of being the first African American to cross boundaries and break barriers to hold the highest office in the land, he felt sort of an affinity to Ms. Destiny Dupree.

Standing to their feet, everyone in attendance began to clap as President Barack Obama, being accompanied by his wife Michelle and his daughters, Sasha and Malia, called for Fatimah and Khadijah to be brought up. Escorted by members of the secret service, their caseworker was honored to accept the awards on their behalf as the medical staff stood with the girls perched in their arms. As Sasha and Malia each handed the caseworker an enlarged plaque, President Obama told the audience that Destiny held the status of a martyr and likened her to the prestigious of Jeannette Rankin, who was the first female U.S. congresswoman. He challenged Fatimah and Khadijah, just as his own daughters were challenged, to surpass the boundaries of the antecedent success of their ancestors.

Beaming with Afrocentric Pride into the faces of the little girls who were barely over a month old, and suffering from the plague of involuntary existence, Michelle hoped that somehow the aspirations of their future would overshadow the calamities of their past. Pulled by the cueing of one of the presidential staff, President Obama closed by taking pictures with the precious little girls and was whisked away to Air Force One.

CHAPTER 5

"**A**ll rise", screamed the bailiff as the judge marched up the aisles of the hollow court room. Entering from the door of her chambers, The Honorable Chastity Kellogg made her way to the high backed chair, and, upon seating herself, tapped her gavel and told the few in attendance that they may be seated. Looking over the rim of her gold framed glasses, while skimming over the docket, she was relieved by the simplicity of the matters being argued before her. Scanning over the seating arrangements, her heart sank to see the twin royal blue bassinets with the attached oxygen machines being attended by two nurses. Clearing her throat, she went through all the legal jargon and got straight to the issue. "We are here to hear the case of: Fatimah and Khadijah Dupree vs. The United States. Which side would like to go first?"

The attorney for the plaintiffs, Charlie M. Peutz, Esquire, jumped to his feet and in a bombing voice started, "I would like to make a motion, Your Honor! This motion is in reference to the United States Navy's intention to withhold the $250,000 insurance payment that these young ladies are entitled to. If you will, Your Honor, I ask that you turn to exhibit one of the the brief that's been submitted. Here you'll find a letter from the Navy Base at which Ms. Dupree was stationed at the time of her passing. The letter is printed on authentic government issued stationary and states … Due to the fact that these young ladies were merely fetuses at the time of Petty Officer Dupree's demise, they intended to contest the rights of these young ladies possible status as beneficiaries. Your Honor, I have here today expert witnesses , who will give their expert testimony under oath that a fetus is, in fact, a living entity and has just as much entitlement to the U.S. Constitution as any other human being. At the end of this argument, I am prepared to ask for a directed verdict.

"Objection, Your Honor! A group of JAG Lawyers had predicted the type of picture that Mr. Peutz would paint in open court and determined amongst themselves, that should he proceed in this fashion, the Navy should recant their claim and grant the deceased officer's children all of their rights protected and due to them under the Uniformed Code of Military Justice. May we approach the bench, Your Honor?"

Shaking her head and motioning in the affirmative, Rear Admiral Jordan and Attorney Peutz walked towards the judge. Upon reaching the bench, the highly decorated naval adjutant asked for a conference in her chambers. Banging her gavel, Judge Kellogg set the court in recess for thirty minutes. Sitting at the head of the mahogany wood table, Rear Admiral Jordan pulled a large manila folder from his briefcase and began explaining the contents.

"Your Honor, on behalf of the United States Navy, the government is prepared to offer Fatimah and Khadijah Dupree not only their entitlement to their mother's insurance policy, but also the full benefits package, which includes but is not limited to, health insurance and dental care—also, military IDs and the use of all the military banking systems. Their lawyer and medical fees will be paid in full, and all of their mother's possessions have been placed into storage until the children are adopted or old enough to take possession for themselves. Be as it may, there is one stipulation that we would ask Attorney Peutz to agree to. That is, that all safekeeping and monetary transactions be conducted by way of the Navy Federal Credit Union. Your Honor, being that Ms. Dupree had been active military since she was eighteen years old and hasn't purchased any property, it is my position to minimize the length and cost of the probate process. Here, I have everything ready to be handed over to Attorney Peutz on his clients behalf. All benefits are active until their eighteenth birthday, unless the twins choose to follow in their mother's footsteps and join the Armed Services of the United States. Copies of everything have been made available for your inspection, Your Honor, and I thank you for allowing me to correct the grave disservice of our previous intent to argue this case in court."

Upon receipt and inspection, Attorney Peutz was satisfied with the outcome of these sudden turn of events. After handing over the freshly printed military IDs and satisfied that all the *T's* were crossed and all the *I's* had been dotted, he assured Judge Kellogg that he was prepared, on behalf of the plaintiffs, to accept the governments offer and discontinue the legal proceedings. Being that this case took on the complex jurisprudence of both military and civilian law. Judge Kellogg felt it in the best interest of all parties involved to make a direct verdict and grant the government's wish to bring this case to a close.

CHAPTER 6

Jazmine Winters, a 10 year tenured veteran of Child Psychology, cruised down Sports Arena Blvd. en route to the dreadful Child Protection Services Agency that was crammed into the corner of the Cineplex in the lot adjacent to Jack Murphy Stadium. Today was the day where the twins would be a separated, and it was eating at the core of her maternal being. After spending a year with Fatimah and Khadijah, the girls were adjusting as well as to be expected without the nurturing and guidance of a mother. As she sat in the car putting all of her personal emotions in check concerning the grave injustice being done to these already troubled children by the system, Jaz took a deep breath, willing her professional nature to kick in.

As she stepped into the congested conference room,

all eyes locked on Ms. Winters—dressed in a sleek and pricey off-white Donna Karen pantsuit, with opened toe matching Ferragamo three-inch heels. Her olfactory senses picked up the mixed scent of lust and hate. Placing the eggshell colored Louis Vuitton briefcase with the peanut butter hued lettering on the table, her appearance commanded both, attention and adoration. Taking her time situating her paperwork, she zoomed into the eyes of every individual present from behind the gold-framed lenses of the prescription Fendi glasses. Biting back the bile that arose in her throat, Jaz simply removed her glasses and sat straight-backed into the chair. Immediately, the high-pitched voice of Mrs. Gloria Klein began making the introductions throughout the room. Obviously displeased at Khadijah and Fatimah being separated, their attorney, Mr. Peutz, openly condemned the decision. While it was true that his oratory skills in a courtroom could sway the minds of judge and jury, this was not a court room, and the verdict had already been passed down. Showing her quiet support, Ms. Winters placed a calming hand on the disorderly lawyer's shoulder. Both girls were being placed into Caucasian families and were being sent to opposite ends of the country. This was distasteful, rude, and downright evil, but hasn't that always been the systematic response to Black families in crisis? To further flaunt the agency's decision, under the cloak of courtesy, the adopting families urged the girl's psychologist to render her final analyses and summation of her findings during her time as their clinical psychologist.

"Foundation being the common denominator in this case, we have to start from the womb. A mother shapes and teaches a child from the time it moves from an embryo and takes the form of a fetus through the biochemistry of her thoughts. With the knowledge of who Ms. Destiny Dupree was, and understanding the hardships with which she encountered that brought about her pregnancy, we can assess by her rigid decision to carry the pregnancy to term, that out of love, she weighed her options. Therefore, from conception the foundation was strong. I am under the professional influence of thought, that they each serve as the others remaining thread of foundation."

"As young traumatic children, continued counseling, care, and the company of one another, along with a nurturing home filled with normalcy, could very well prove to be conducive to their plight. Both Fatimah and Khadijah have abnormally high intelligence quotients, thus, making them child prodigies in their own right. They are very codependent and overly protective of one another and are sticklers for neatness and order. However, I find the incorrigible facts that both girls have elevated mean streaks when separated for great lengths of time, are each very defensive of their own personal space, and neither child smiles much or finds many things that most kids find amusing. What befuddles me the most as a child psychologist, is their attraction, not only as children, but as little girls, toward the mystery of how things work as opposed to playing with them. It is my final conclusion that the child protection agency is doing these girls a grave disservice by separating them for the purpose of closing a case file. Separation will minimize any chances they have of establishing emotional and psychological footing. Ultimately, you are severing their need for devotion and loyalty to each other.

Feeling berated and a little defensive, caseworker Klein had to rebut Ms. Winters direct attack against her humanity. "Ms. Winters, personally, I value your opinion. You have served as an invaluable asset to this agency over the decade you have been working with us. However, I think you would agree that it would serve as an greater injustice to shuffle these brilliant minds through the foster care system, for Lord knows how long it could take to find a home for the both of them that's economically suitable. It is my job as their caseworker to process the paperwork for the most all-around stable environment for any case that I'm assigned, and I'll be the first to admit that separating Fatimah and Khadijah Dupree is not the most fashionable alternative. Be as it may, CPS has been forced to choose between the lesser of two evils. Thank you for your advice and observation. I ask both families to follow me to the reception area so that we may conclude the adoption process and close the case of Fatimah and Khadijah Dupree."

CHAPTER 7

When I die, fuck it, I wanna go to hell

'cause I'm a piece of shit, it ain't hard to fucking tell.

It don't make sense going to heaven

with the goody goodies

dressed in white, I like black

Timbs and black hoodies.

God will probably have me on some real strict shit,

no sleeping all day, no getting my dick licked.

Hanging with the goody goodies, lounging in paradise-

fuck that shit—I wanna tote guns and shoot dice.

All my life I been considered as the worst,

lying to my mother, even stealing her purse.

Crime after crime, from drugs to extortion,

I know she wish she had a fucking abortion…

Fatimah had her eyes closed, allowing the words of *Suicidal Thoughts* from Biggie Smalls, *Ready To Die* album enhance her state of cogitation to the point of being hypnotized. Never fully understanding how evolution could be so cruel and give her life, despite her objection to live, she constantly tip-toed across the tightrope of suicidal and homicidal thoughts. Deciding to act out her thought process in alphabetical order until she felt justice was served, she would play her position.

After eight years of suppressing her hunger for revenge, it stood only inches from her fingertips. The walls of the Super 8 Motel in New London, Connecticut, was the after hours rendezvous of the sailors and students at the submarine base in Groton. After spending a week in the same room and frequenting the NCO Club nightly, Fatimah had been passed off as just another pretty face in uniform. Quickly making company with a group of Sack-Chasers known as The Poison Clan, she learned how to amalgamate into her environment. Her days were spent perusing the humongous Navy Exchange. Suddenly, her patience paid off. "Excuse me, Miss," came from the chapped lips of a short, stumpy, and highly decorated officer as he bumped her from behind. Most would call it luck, but in this case, it was considered *destiny*. As their eyes locked, Fatimah had a premonition that this man was the cause of her curse standing right in front of her in human form. But it wasn't until her eyes roamed and glanced the shiny insignia of an golden anchor and two stars.. Could it be? Flinching as she pronounced the name to herself, she felt the sudden urge to release her bowels. Coaxing herself to calm down and not overplay her hand, Fatimah excused herself, hurrying to find the ladies room as Master Chief Cox's features sketched themselves into her mind. Normally, atheists don't believe in divine intervention, but today, Heaven opened up and handed her an angel. Watching her ass as she walked in the opposite direction, he was hooked. Ever since the undercover operation in Somalia so long ago, Chief Cox seemed to be trapped on the dark side. Glancing over her shoulder, Fatimah smiled 'cause soon he would realize that ... *once you go black, you never go back!*

Catching up to the 5 ft 7 in gorgeous black girl with the flawless complexion, the color of tarnished bronze, he asked if she was a student or if Groton was her permanent duty station. Playing the well-rehearsed role, Fatimah ex-plained that she had recently arrived to her new duty station and still had a few days of leave left before she had to report. So far, she had only been able to find her way to the Exchange and back to her motel at the Super 8. The sparkle in his eyes revealed his perverted lust as he began to flaunt his credentials. Hoping to impress the "fresh meat", he invited her on a tour of the simulated submarine, since women were not yet assigned to sub duty. Jumping at the opportunity, Fatimah listened intently while he gave her directions and pointed to the small building just up the hill from the parking lot, telling her to meet him there at seventeen hundred hours. She knew this would give her just enough time to check out of the room rented under a false identity and put her plan together.

Slowly slipping the elastic of her pants over the curve of her perfectly rounded ass, the glow from the candles danced off the walls creating the intimate atmosphere that was intended. Laying under the covers enjoying the strip tease and waiting on her husband to walk through the door, Maxine was pleased with herself. Standing at almost 5 ft 8 in, with the body of a professional fitness trainer with skin as smooth as ice and the color of oven-baked clay, along with facial features that would guarantee the cover of any magazine, Khadijah was definitely a dollar swimming in a sea of dimes. Pulling the covers back, Maxine's big pink nipples stood up like miniature bullets as she squirmed her tanned body around with two of her fingers frantically working the inside of her vagina and her thumb stimulating her clit. Crawling between her parted thighs, Khadijah began to lick and suck at the finger going in and out of her rose pink essence. Moving the thumb away from her clit with her tongue, Khadijah began nibbling and nipping at her oversized gland. Just as Maxine Robblier's body started to tremble, the twist of the door knob was heard just above her moans. The Marine intelligence officer didn't take a moment to think … seeing the mahogany butt cheeks spread wide like eagle's wings and the pussy just as thick, dripping juices like a ripened peach peeking back at him, he began coming out of his clothes at the door.

Being a main course lesbian with the occasional fetish for dick, Khadijah was having the "best of both worlds" as Rob slid inside of her from behind. Since he crawled up behind her, taking sexual instruction from a dog, in the end he would be treated like one. Just when he thought he was going to cum, Khadijah bucked her powerful hips backwards, just hard enough to knock her victim off balance, and with Mach speed, she rolled to her left, swinging the baby machete in an expert fashion thus emasculating him in the blink of an eye. Putting patches of napalm on the places where her DNA may be left on the dying man's body, she ended his misery by snapping his neck. The damage had been done before his wife even registered what had taken place. She pointed the huge weapon in her face and stated, "Bitch, you better not scream." Laughing the whole while, Khadijah grabbed the testicles off the bed. "Maxine, you seduced me so good, I think you earned your honorary pair of nuts." She tossed them in her lap, causing Maxine to flinch back from the flesh. Khadijah shot her square between the eyes. Placing General Robblier's body on the bed, she said, "I now pronounce you man and wife" as she set the napalm on fire.

CHAPTER 8

It's easier getting into military installations around the world than it is getting into liquor stores in large cities. The lackadaisical running of Uncle Sam would definitely cost the Department of Defense $250,000 worth of insurance money today. Fatima seemed happy as she pranced up the hill towards the building which contained the submarine simulations. Dressed in a black mini skirt, showing off her toned legs and thighs, with a matching black spandex midriff top caressing a pair of perky grapefruit sized breasts and a black drawstring bag over her shoulder, she opted for the college schoolgirl look. Stepping up to the oversized glass door, she inspected herself in the squeaky clean mirror-like glass. She found it amusing that she was indeed armed and dangerous and in an unorthodox fashion, dressed to kill.

Holding back excitement, Master Chief Cox was elated to see fresh meat waiting for him at the door. Licking his lips as he inspected this goddess, taking the view in from her size four black and white Air Force Ones, all the way to the set of sculptured cheekbones that once upon a time was a prerequisite for beauty. Letting her in, he to a chance to look into those sparkling brown eyes and would have traded in his career for some of this "prime black pussy". Leading her into a room with what looked to be the huge frame of a gutted out go-kart, he went about the business of explaining how the simulator worked and what it was designed to teach. From the way he kept devouring her with his eyes, they might as well have been in the booth of a Mexican brothel. Taking her seat beside him in the thingamajig, the name of the contraption having slipped her mind, noticing there were two awkward looking steer-ing wheels—or should she say controls, Master Chief be-gan to carefully explain that one control determined the degrees, and the control on her side, controlled the depth. As if teaching a child to ride a bike, he took pride in this training. Not quite catching on to the workings of this whole submarine bullshit, Fatimah started going with her control. She noticed that every time she pulled it up, the simulator angled upward and when she pushed the control downward the machine tilted that way; she started to comprehend the meaning. Giving Fatimah the ultimate feel of being in control, it kind of reminded her of having sex in the missionary position where the man controlled how shallow or how deep he went inside of her. Pulling her control all the way up, her skirt rode high on her hips, flashing the print of her pussy for Cox to see. He reached over to cop a feel, comfortable that he had her wrapped up in his display. She put her hand on top of his and guided it to the puff in her panties. Being the disciplined man that he was, he didn't like that she had changed the flow of control. He had to have it on his terms. Knowing the insinuation he was making, he said, "Now that you understand at least how the depth controller works, how about we do an emergency blow?" Seeing and sensing her anger, Master Chief Cox amusingly explained that an emergency blow was a procedure used by emptying the ballast tanks, to get a submarine unsubmerged in a hurry. This procedure can be mandated by a few circumstances, underwater mountains, enemy subs, or anything of that nature. Totally taken by his student, he brushed off a faint sound, as if a screw had come a loose and bolts were rattling. He'd have it checked out in the morning; all he want-ed to do now was… "Oh shit!" It felt like he had been stung all around his ankles by a thousand little bees. Jumping a few feet from the moving simulator, he saw baby petioles hanging from his skin. "You little bitch!" He screamed and started moving toward Fatimah, however, she knew that within the scope of sixty seconds, the venom of the Bohemian Baby Cottonmouths would start to shut down his nervous system.

Slipping to an early death, Master Chief Cox could have sworn he saw the female version of the devil. The last words he ever heard were "Payback for the last operation in Somalia!" *Just like that mission, even though it didn't literally kill Destiny, was never validated or affirmed by good ole Uncle Sam, neither will the soul of Master Chief Cox,* thought Fatimah, as she whispered in his ear… "See you in Hell, mother fucker!!!"

CHAPTER 9

Sitting in the back of the limo, riding down Washington Road en route to the Augusta National Golf Club, Khadijah was going over her account statements and saw where her deposit was made. Closing the file folder, she was amazed at just how fond of James Brown country she had become. Being close enough to the National where she could play every day of the season was an added bonus. As the limo was ushered into the security of the most beautiful golf course in the world, Khadijah got misty-eyed as she took in all of its opulence and had thoughts of her mother on her mind. As she was escorted through the club house, the general manager of daily operations, Mr. D. Spencer, Augusta's very own David Dukes if ever there was one—she could feel the hate and disdain exuding through his pores. He didn't realize that hate is what made her. *God forbid someone ever puts a price on his head!* Dressed in a pink Baby Phat tennis skirt, a pair of white leather Foot Joy golf spikes, an all white Masters tee, and a matching pink Baby Phat visor, Khadijah showed off her fabulous figure to the group of white women who came from a very long bloodline of "old money." This included Tiffany Shula, daughter of previous Miami Dolphins head coach, Sheila Wynn, daughter of Steve Wynn—owner of the chain of Wynn Resort Hotels, Georgia Mae Jones, daughter of redneck extraordinaire and golf guru, Mr. Late Bobby Jones, and Regina Ford, daughter of the man behind the migration, Mr. Henry Ford III, owner of the Ford Motor Company.

Khadijah, being the only black person besides her caddy, Junior, who was featured in the Augusta National Caddy Hall of Fame, was treated with the dignity of a pet poodle at these events. Even so, it was her one chance to display her prestige and status in the face of the genera-tionally rich, and every time she bent over her putty stick, her skirt rose just high enough to signal in the face of prej-udism that he could kiss her black ass! Pillow talk was that Khadijah Dupree was just as remarkable as the fathers of the women that she played golf with. Except she was a little more… "rough around the edges." In this level of life, influence checks affluence and money respects money, but it's definitely nice to have a problem solver on the team, so long as the problem solver never becomes the problem.

Teaming with her closest friend, Khadijah and Georgia Mae were in the lead at the third round. As Junior studied the twelve foot distance, dictating angle and measuring the wind, Georgia Mae asked Khadijah, "Why do you stick to your profession?" Moving as if the question had never been presented, Junior whispered in Khadijah's ear and handed her the club. With the concentration of a Buddhist monk, she cocked the putty club back about eight inches. With a smooth follow-through, the ball went to the right. With the accuracy of a professionally shot cue-ball, it merged left and landed home for the birdie. Straight-legged, Khadijah bent over to pick up her tee, and necks turned crimson red as the message of the trim of her thong, disappearing between the cheeks of her perfectly rounded ass, was clearly felt. Moving with a large lead towards the fourth round of play, whispers were made in the stands about the negro girl who would walk away with millions of hard working "white folks money". As the last hole was played, Junior snatched Khadijah and Georgia Mae's bags so they could take pictures and receive their awards. With the bright flash from cameras and the noise from the clapping of the crowd erupting loudly, Khadijah put her arm around her partner and whispered, "Just look around you; the world is run by dogs, and to them we are just two more female Pit-Bulls in a skirt—long as we don't piss in their yards, they couldn't care less who we cock our legs up to, down the block."

CHAPTER 10

The Navy Criminal Investigative Service (NCIS), was swarming the submarine base in Groton, CT. Master Chief Cox's body lay stiff and swollen in the chalk-line, creating a mounting rage through commissioned officers world wide. The United States Military served as the primary recruiting camp for those who liked to operate in clandestine circles.

Pus and, what discovery would soon show to be poisonous venom, oozed from the porous skin surrounding the dead man's ankles, causing his feet to appear as if they were breathing. With no clues, motives, or suspects, the Military Police started tagging and bagging the evidence and removed the spectacle of the body to be autopsied, so they could find out the cause of death. Standing at the back of the now fading crowd, a highly decorated black officer kneeled beside Wendy Shields, the lead Navy Criminal Investigative Officer, and whispered something in her ear that drained the color from her already pale face. "How do you know," she asked? "Because I just buried a soldier in the Afghan Desert from a poisonous snake bite! I'm not an investigator, and I don't want to infringe on your duties—but from the location and the tiny diameter of the holes, I'm willing to bet you a billion dollars to a bucket of shit, they were baby snakes! "This is no coincidence, this is murder!" "How can you be so definitive in that assessment Chief..?" "Williams, Eric William's the name."

"Well Mrs. Shields, if you look at both legs carefully, you can see a bunch of tiny red spots. This is where the fangs of maybe a dozen or so baby poisonous snakes penetrated the flesh." Confused, she asked, "Why would someone want to commit murder taking the chance of using baby snakes?" Unsettled by the criminal investigators ignorance, Chief Williams sarcastically remarked, "In order to ensure the job was done." The thing about baby snakes is they can't control their venom, making the kill swift and accurate. Although it take one cold-hearted, son-of a-bitch to watch the work of the devil for the roughly sixty seconds it takes for the venom to shut down the nervous system, It's a clean kill. It leaves no traceable evidence—no fingerprints, no DNA or hair follicles. But, it does take a seasoned herpetologist to release and recover the snakes without being laid to rest right beside him. And, for the record Mrs. Shields, even though you may never capture the killer, you just gained knowledge that's invaluable in nature."

Meanwhile, just four states over from the pandemonium in which she left behind, Fatimah stood crouched down next to the grave marker of her mother. The wind was constant at the Arlington National Cemetery, and she noticed she was the only visitor of the day. She placed the vase of fresh flowers on Destiny's marker. Sitting cross-legged beside the grave, Fatimah started talking to the spirit of her mother, as usual. "Destiny, why would you bring us into this world under such disturbed and wretched conditions? I know you had no control over the time frame of your life, but love was the one chemical that was absent from our genetics. I'm sure, had you lived, you would have overcompensated us in that department, but how can I show or have love, when it's never been shown or given to me? All that you left for me to love was stripped away before I ever even learned to say my own name. I didn't come to make this a pity party. I came to tell you that your honor is finally starting to be avenged. Even though you survived, it was by design for you to die out there in the jungles of Africa. Although you beat the odds, Chief Cox didn't get that lucky. I don't know if me and Khadijah will ever be reunited. So much time has lapsed, and with each day that passes, it only widens the gap of probability. But every time I get sick out of the blue, or catch pains for no apparent reason, the passing of telepathy between us keeps me optimistic. Hopefully, it will happen sooner than later 'cause I'm losing hope fast! I need my other half to free me from this curse. In departing, if ever love did exist, I'm sure it's in the form of my tears, that come annually on these visits. Precipitation is my only way of expressing an emotion I've never known. See you in January!

CHAPTER 11

Handing Khadijah the confirmation of her partial deposit, her contractor asked, really not expecting an answer, "What's your fascination and apparent disdain for men in uniform?" Taking insult, she corrected him, "Service men, let's get it right, or you just may make a payment for a contract that I refuse to fill." Smiling deviously, she said, "And I guess you would want a refund?" Turning stone cold, Khadijah explained herself. Service men think being in uniform removes from them the ramifications of murder.They have no regard for the action, but what about the reaction that nature deems to be equal, or greater to, in return? Besides that they are fraternal twins to convicts, they both feed off the umbilical cord of institutionalization. "Creatures of habit and repetition always make for easy prey." Being a woman, all I have to do is wait until the time of peace, throw them the promise of pussy, and it's a wrap. It called The Pavlov Effect—they are conditioned like dogs. Every time a woman opens her legs and displays the bowl, he will stick his head in and eat. "Now, if you don't mind, you can hand me the profile and excuse yourself so I can get back to my book." A fan of urban literature, Khadijah was reading part two of Bishop, called: The Bulldog Crew," by Alfred Adams, Jr. (AKA: SHABORN). Her insides started to tingle due to her attraction to the imaginary character, Devine. *My girl Wahida Clark got it wrong when she said "Every thug needs a lady." If truth be told it's the other way around—every lady needs a thug! No matter if she's black, white, intelligent, or ignorant, every woman secretly has a sweet tooth for that strong, black, smart, thugged-out, rugged, and loyal mandingo."* The two main characters, Bishop and Devine, made a unique team in an unorthodox way—kind of like hearing a remix of Kirk Franklin featuring Jada Kiss… Now tell me that ain't power in prayer!

CHAPTER 12

Crossing the threshold of his sanctuary, Ensign Cedric Vinson smelled the fading scent of his wife's favorite perfume. Although the smell of *Butterfly*, by Mariah Carey, was high in the air, underneath it lingered that fury, a ripe, rich, and dangerous odor that put him on alert. After searching the house, room by room, with his weapon at the ready, he passed the feeling off as a sense of paranoia. Holstering the service issued .45, Ensign Vinson, who'd recently graduated the Office Training Academy at the Naval Training Center in San Diego, removed his peacoat. Ignoring the chill hanging at the base of his neck and prematurely descending from the crescendo of fear, his eyes grew to the diameter of silver half dollars as the searing sensation of the stun gun sizzled through the military creases of his dress uniform.

Barely a day past being a baby, Khadijah couldn't help but be reminded of the character, Bishop, from the book she'd just finished reading. Cinnamon brown smooth skin, close cropped wavy hair, body tight and trim, with just a hint of a dimple touching his cheek, she figured they should have been somewhere making life instead of his being taken. "Too bad his number has been called!" Using a combination of slip knots to tie the victim. Whomever's toes he had stepped on still held the grudge, and paid for the payback to be as painful as possible. While waiting on her mark to regain consciousness, Khadijah slipped into the black latex cat-suit and matching gloves. Looking at the pictures of he and his wife spread out over the huge bedroom, she knew that his gorgeous looks would be the last thing he would be remembered for.

Blindfolded and gagged, Ensign Vinson came to and could only listen for sound. In this present state, he couldn't move; all he could do was anticipate his fate. A smooth, quick, back-hand slap across his face got his attention. The hurt came more from not seeing it coming. "Mr. Vinson, you obviously offended the wrong people this time," came the sexy, soft and calculated voice of a woman; who without warning slapped the holy shit out of her victim again, snatching the blindfold from his tearful eyes, she noticed a pool of blood, snot, and tears forming a line from his nose to the tape covering his mouth. *Guess men really do cry in the dark, huh? Okay, Mr. Vinson, you are indeed a beautiful brotha, but this is the game of torture. By the time your pathetic life comes to an end, your extraordinarily good looks will have irreversibly gotten uglier.* A round house to the face left his nose lopsided and broken. Turning, she spied the bulge of his eyes as she ran the serrated blade of the knife over the open flame of a makeshift torch. Even in pain and at the prospect of death, Ced couldn't stop glancing at her ass straining against the latex.

"Tell me, Mr. Vinson, how many ways are there to skin a man and keep him alive?" With the red glow from the blade, she sliced lightly from jaw-bone to his cheek and snatched the skin roughly from his face. Pink slowly fading to crimson red, Khadijah smashed the butt of the knife against the patch of tape where one lip met with the other. Taking a break, she left the room, leaving Ensign Vinson to stare at himself in the full-sized mirror. Coming back into the room with a hand-held mirror, he jumped at the sound of her footsteps. Traumatized and still holding out hope, it all quickly faded as she smashed the mirror into his face. Finally when he passed out, she poured a glass of cold water onto his face, bringing him out of his state of unconsciousness where he had found his comfort zone. As his stilled-smoky brown eyes focused on the lifeless spaces that occupied her eyes sockets, he knew it was over… As she opened him up from ear to ear.

CHAPTER 13

Upon completing her bi-annual training in the hills of Afghanistan, Fatimah was giver her most dangerous assignment yet. If she ever forgot, or diverted, from her teachings, that would be the most fatal mistake she would ever make! The two-headed Rock Viper was the only one of its kind, the rarest snake in the world, and as of to date, also the most deadliest. For quite a few reasons, the snake was unique in its character. Being that it had two heads, it moved at speeds of up to twenty miles per hour, could strike in any position and in any direction, and also moved in the side-winding motion toward its intended victim. Sunflower yellow, it had streaks of vermillion diamond patterned designs. There was no cure for it's bite and no known serum to stop the process of it's venom. Storing the makeshift fiberglass carrying case, Fatimah retreated to her quarters to pack her things for the twenty hour flight back to San Antonio, Texas. After freshening up and gathering all her belongings, she sat to study her next target. Going over the floor plans of the house, she came up with an idea to minimize the dangers she faced. Learning that the victim had a one-year-old daughter, and his wife was recently deceased due to a car wreck, wickedly, the vision of her debauchery started to form in her mind. While taking in the dusty scenery from the back windows of the limousine, Fatimah and the contractor broached the issue of payment. Knowing how fickle and creative she could be when it came to her compensation, he knew it would require a great deal of strategy, time, and money to meet her demands. Although, her contractor was also the man that raised her, how could she ever trust the motherfucker who turned her into a demon? Staring at him through steely deep brown eyes, Fatimah was convinced that race was obsolete, and only two types of people existed—*the mutha fuckers and the muther fucked*. If she adopted the title of the mutha fucker, what did that make the bastard sitting beside her? Catching the murderous gleam in her eyes, the contractor knew that he would eventually be presented with the fruits of his labor.

Just when it was thought that the "devil's progeny" couldn't outdo her last set of demands, Fatimah opened up Pandora's Box. It appeared that she had a sixth sense for making her demands of payment just as dangerous as the actual job itself. Meticulous at covering her tracks, she never talked about a job and the payment on the same day… and she never, ever accepted currency unless it came in the form of rare coins. *What good is the Almighty Dollar when you can't spend it?* she used to wonder. The true Capitalist that she was, Fatimah learned that only the truly rich controlled the natural resources!

As the Limo pulled up to the private airstrip next to the luxurious GSJ-V, Fatimah became almost jovial in nature. Handing the contractor a piece of paper, she told him to log onto the website for an auction. Up for sale was one of Leonardo Davinci's original sketch pads. Since she couldn't own the regional painting of the Mona Lisa, then the original Sketch was the next best thing. She informed him that the bidding started at $150,000. Her departing instructions were the most surprising. "Here's a number to some personal friends of mine in Libya. They are the sons of Muammar Qadaffi, and they own the diamond mines all over Northern Africa. I need two, sixteen ounce, untreated, raw diamonds from their mines. They will contact me when the purchase is made. Last, but not least, you have to pay to play. I will be waiting on the certificates of authentication for both—the sketch and the raw diamonds.

Just a warning, be careful when dealing with the Qadhaffis, they are extremely militant and have a strong distaste for white men." Smiling, Fatimah grabbed her bags and ascended the makeshift stairs, boarding the comfort of the Gulf Stream Jet.

CHAPTER 14

Legs akimbo, poised in the two-handed Weaver Stance, Khadijah held firmly to the Heckler and Koch MP5. Lightweight and easy to handle, this weapon was ideal for her choosing. The tin target formed the shape of a human body's upper torso and she barely moved as every round landed in the range from the chin to directly between the eyes. The Fort Gordon Firing Range was one of Khadijah Dupree's many training facilities. The recoil of rapid fire from weapons ranging In size from .22 caliber hand guns to M-16 military-issued assault rifles, caused a steady vibration of deadly hums to chorus through the air. Her small arms instructor, Master Sergeant Travis Brown, had taken a special interest in his student. Despite her pulchritude, he appreciated her precocious nature and took no precautions in imparting his expertise and wisdom where firearms were concerned.

Perfecting the art of firing handguns ambidextrously, Khadijah seemed to mentally, as well as physically, prepare herself for any situation. After shooting exercises concluded, they went to the classroom for the drills of breaking down and interchanging parts of certain handguns simultaneously. This came as an added bonus to being able to pick a mans brains from fifteen yards away. Ending the two minute breakdown drills, she stowed her weapon in its carrying case and exited the building. Hopping into the sleek Pearl Blue CLK-400 Benz, Khadijah dropped the top, as she made her way through gate number five. Dean's Bridge Road was fairly empty as she navigated the cross-town trek to the Augusta Mall. Giving a lot of thought lately to her chosen profession, she needed to pick up something nice to wear.

CHAPTER 15

Holding the Quran that her trainer and dear friend, Prince Fazaad Ali, had given to her during her last training session in Saudi Arabia, Khadijah couldn't believe that she was taking him up on his offer to change her life. Trusting her friend, trainer, and confidant, completely had paid off. In her hands, she held the keys of financial freedom. Prince Ali had a long arm's reach within the Muslim world and extended his compassionate hand from the deserts of Arabia to the desolation of Illinois.

While studying the words written in Arabic, the cab driver wasted no time getting her from the humongous O'Hare International Airport to 79th and Stoney Island. Not at all what she was expecting, or accustomed to, while training in Saudi Arabia, the mosque took up over half the block. Pulling up on the opposite side of the street, to the

accounting office of Malik A. Rafsanjani, Khadijah was excited to have found a prospect who was capable of undertaking a task of this magnitude. After paying and tip-
ping the driver, he peeled off as though the streets were
going to erupt into flames at any moment. She would
later learn that the South Side of Chicago had that kind
of reputation. Once inside the plush office, which served
as a contradiction to the plain structure of bland bricks
on the outside, she instantly became fascinated by all of
the Islamic and African inspired art. While she inspected
the thorough craftsmanship of the bright, multi-colored
prayer rug that hung high up on a wall, a man with the
same build and a similar facial structure as the late Malcolm X, invited her into his office. Expecting her, Malik was
under the impression by her name that she was also of
the faith. Greeting her in normal Islamic fashion, "A salaam
alaikum," he instantly realized from her expression, that
she was not a Muslimah as he originally assumed. Signal-
ing her to have a seat in the plush leather chair, he moved
around to the business end of the oak desk.

Before any business could be conducted, Khadijah
asked if there was a restroom that she could use. After
rinsing her hands off, she returned to reclaim her seat.

Upon sitting down, she reached into her large handbag and handed Mr. Rafsanjani the thick leather bounded Quran. This shocked him. She responded, "Your services come highly recommended by a personal friend of mine. If you will, Prince Fazaad Ali asked me to direct you to the inside cover. He said that you would understand." The message was written in Arabic, and by his reaction, he was obviously elated and awed by the contents. In Mr. Rafsanjani's eyes was an almost conspiratorial glaze that she could not comprehend. Wanting to conduct her business and get away from the pull of attraction that the moisture pooling in her panties was evidence of, Khadijah pulled her portfolio out and placed it on the desk. Studying his every facial reaction as he perused the contents of the numbered accounts, she was becoming assured that she had been led in the right direction. "Ms. Dupree, you have a very complex problem, however, I believe there may be options that will basically borderline a solution. In return for undertaking his recommendation and due to the fact of your valued friendship, I have been advised by Prince Ali to accommodate your financial needs and desires using all means available. This includes, but is not limited to, the option of using the Royal Bank of Arabia to keep your identity and actual holdings concealed. The process is rather simple and expedient, due to the fact that it will be, or can be, handled through what we call an iInternational money transfer. Because this transaction is conducted through countries rather than individuals, and has the stamp of approval by the IMF (International Monetary Fund), your identity remains anonymous. However, I believe the biggest perk you'll find is that your money is 100% insured. Ms. Dupree, I am also advised to be the bearer of bad news. This offer is conditional." A smile etching the corners of his lips, "Prince Fazaad Ali counseled me to extend to you this offer with the counter-offer that you allow me to introduce you to Islam." Knowing that she should have anticipated this from her humble friend, she reached to shake Mr. Rafsanjani's hand and said to him, "Please advise Prince Ali that I accept, but only with the understanding that this will simply be an introduction and not a conversion!"

CHAPTER 16

A sunny day in San Antonio warranted a stroll down the board walk. Seeing the strange man sitting on the bench, under most circumstances, would have been a cause for alarm, but to the contrary, this stranger was a sight for sore eyes. As instructed and paid to do, no words were passed, only goods and orders were exchanged. As soon as Fatimah distributed the diamonds and sketch pad to her safety deposit box, she would be on the way to cause chaos in central Corpus Christi.

There was a prominent Jewish community situated in the comfortable military town. Jews tended to make their dwellings in the center of middle class America. Being the media gods of the world, they relished the safety and simplicity of the middle margins between class consciousness. Americans seemed to love them more than their fellow citizens. Benson Leopold, better known in the hood as "Big L," was considered an icon amongst the youth of this relatively small city. Owning and operating most of the jewelry stores in town, he catered to the hip-hop generations scheme of style. Being known to slash prices, adjusting to his customer's economic capabilities, and the fact that his family has been in business here for three decades-exempted from the madness that Jews only media liked. The two and a half hour drive from San Antonio to Corpus Christi, Texas, seemed as if it only took thirty minutes to conquer. The adrenaline rush of earning her keep was equivalent to a sexual climax. That deep void in space, where time, colors, and craters collide, causing a gastric explosion sending everything into the abstract abyss, somewhere between paradise and heaven. Crossing the long bridge into the Corpus Christi city limits, Fatimah punched the address into the all black Jaguar XK8s navigation system and followed the directions. Known for her splurging on the extra amenities of life, "Big-L's" three story brick house was explored after his death with fascination by his neighbors. The basement level's life-size aquarium was a ten-by-twelve foot aquatic haven for the lover of the submerged species. Made from a wall of five and one-half inch thick architectural safety tempered glass, the aquarium housed exotic fish ranging in size from: the palm of an infants hand to that of a small child. Nothing seemed out of place when the local pool and spa filter truck pulled around back to change the water in the tank and put new filters in. As millions of dollars of fish, with names that most educated people can't even pronounce, were being suctioned into the trucks 10,000 gallon tank, the retractable roof was opened up to reveal the professional plumbing. As the last of the contents had been drained from the over-sized fish tank, Benson Leopold's body was tied pendulously from the piping above. With two accomplices manipulating the length of the rope hanging from the rafters, Fatimah entered the basement with one-year-old Destiny Leopold. Obviously amused that the girl's father was literally hanging in the balance, the child was none the wiser, that today her daddy would pay for the sins of his father—and so would she!

Unconscious and oblivious to what was going on, Fatimah worked diligently to have the stage set when Big L finally came to. Releasing a crater of Australian Androctonus, also known as Fat-Tailed Scorpions, into the sand remaining on the aquariums floor, the final scene had been set for the main event. Although, only a couple of centimeters in size, these scorpions are considered lethal to humans due to the quantity of venom they inject into their victims. Just as Mr. Leopold was coming to, his body was lowered to just inches above the constant whirring and whistling of the striking of arachnid tails. Kneeling beside Destiny, Fatimah pointed at her daddy and asked if she was ready to have some fun. Clapping with childish excitement, Destiny seemed awed as the strobe lights went dark.

Producing the flare gun she brought along for special affects, to animate the whole gruesome act, Fatimah pulled the trigger. *Whoosh*. The blinding glare of the flames jolted Benson into full consciousness. Catching only the silhouette of the two bodies in his peripheral vision, he hadn't yet realized that his whole world was about to come crashing down around him. As she squeezed the trigger once more, the illumination from the pyrotechnic gave off the visage of Fatima and baby Destiny walking through flames. Staring at the Negro girl dressed in all black, smiling sinisterly while holding his daughters hand, the picture of perdition before his eyes reminded him of the Holocaust. Shaking vigorously against that binds that lowered him sanctimoniously to his fate, slowly the tears of realization began to roll in slow motion. It was then that Benson Leopold came to the conclusion that all his life he had been railroaded by religion, and even the confessions and hail Marys couldn't save him nor the only living human that he loved. Cursing the nigger bitch's existence and the middle passage that brought her, he forested all of his cultural religious teachings. Remembering the conversation where someone told him in reference to atrocities that almost destroyed the entire Jewish race, the words pitched forward like a fast ball across the mound of his mind. "Those who deny God could be every bit as wicked and calculating as those who wage war in his name!" Finally resigning himself to his untimely end, Benson Leopold's greed would cause him to meet the only men he respected—dead presidents! Easing the light-weight military sanctioned K-Bar knife from behind her back, Fatimah granted him the agony of torture as she snatched baby Destiny's head back by her blond, curly locks and dragged her to the clear glass so her father could see the fear in her eyes.

Trying to induce an emotion, he asked, "Why harm an innocent child?" Fatimah answered, "Come on Big L, you're westernized now, I know you are familiar with the term 'collateral damage'. She's just a casualty of war. In your faith, you believe in sacrifices, no?" Lifting Destiny's chin up, she sliced upward from the little girls navel until the sharp, serrated blade lodged into the bone of her skull. Using her psychotic sense of humor, Fatiman congratulated him on being shepherdized.

"Officially, you have just lead the sheep into slaughter." Grabbing the limp and lifeless body of Destiny by her tiny ankle, she hoisted the body upside-down and said, "After all, Jews like their meat kosher, don't they?" Tossing the body into the tank, the thousands of arachnids immediately attacked. Nodding her head in the affirmative, Leopold was released and his body dropped next to his deceased daughter. Pulling her to him, he made the sign of the cross over her corpse and stared the female monster dead in the eyes as the venom eased its way into his bloodstream. The whisper of a thousand scorpion tails slicing through the air and piercing human flesh, painted the most evil and vile picture of death that one could ever want to witness. However, Fatimah returned Benson Leopold's stare and mocked his religious gestures by reciprocating the sign of the cross over her chest.

CHAPTER 17

The meeting place was mutual, but his wealth of information was much needed. Khadijah looked delectable in her form fitting, knee-length Marina Rinaldi jersey fabric dress. Accentuated with a pair of Via Spiga blocked open toe sandals, she showed off her perfectly pedicured feet. Heads turned as she strutted through the double doors of the Carter G. Woodson Library to meet Mr. Malik A. Rafsanjani. Stopping at the information desk, the librarian pointed her to a quiet corner from which Malik's gaze emitted. On the sturdy wooden table sat an assortment of books, accompanied by her financial portfolio and the big leather bound Quran, which she recognized as the gift she'd forwarded to him the last time she'd visited Chicago. Unable to deny the mutual pull of attraction between them, Khadijah sat nervously under the microscope of Malik's

open appraisal. Breaking through the fog of unadulter-
ated lust, he silently quoted Surah to break him from his
present train of thoughts, finding the safety net in the finances of this gorgeous goddess before him. He began
spreading the paperwork and forms to be filled out on the
table. Going through the motions of transferring her account from one bank to another, Malik outlined his stocks
and investments and started to explain the different ways
to inflate her net worth. After all, he was her accountant,
wasn't he? Puzzled, Mr. Rafsanjani wasn't sure if he had
been placed on the pay roll, or if this was just pro bono
work as a favor for his Muslim Brother from the world of
Arabia. Time would reveal all things; at the moment, his
focus was getting Khadijah's permission to go ahead in
proceeding with the transfer, then pushing business to
the side so that he could get up close and personal with
this gorgeous sister! Interest rates and amenities were the
straws that broke the camels back for Khadijah.

"Where do I sign?" Not only was she satisfied that this
was indeed the way to go, she was secretly anxious to learn
more about Malik, the man, even if it did mean learning
Malik, the Muslim. Organizing the files and putting everything back into its original order, Mr. Rafsanjani pushed it

towards Ms. Dupree. Although, no specifics had ever been discussed, she picked the folder up and told him, "Correct me if I'm wrong, but every businessman keeps a file for their clients?" Smiling like he had just hit the lottery, Malik basked in the glow of victory. One small battle had been won, but in the time of peace, always prepare for war!

After hours of sitting at the wooden table, Khadijah excused herself to go to the ladies room. Once the door finally slammed shut, she let out the breath she had been holding inside. Whisking her bangs to the side of her eyebrows, she sprayed the insides of her wrist with just a dab of Channel No. 5 that she kept in the form of a travel bottle. Winking at herself in the mirror, she gave a little pep talk, "Ok, Khadijah, it's now or never." Forcing back the butterflies, she caught the stares of every man studying in the building on her way back to the table. Keeping his eyes on the prize, Malik pictured this sheer essence of beauty walking towards him down the aisle at their wedding. Damn, she was fine! Feeling her heart flutter as she neared the table, Khadijah was disappointed to see everything put away, except a single book of some sort. As she sat down and pushed her chair up to the table, Malik came around and took the seat next to her. "I know this is supposed to be our time for me to introduce you to Islam, however, I first want to introduce you to the beauty of yourself." Deeply inhaling her scent, what he really wanted to do was make love to her, and send her back to Georgia to pack her bags. Looking into her eyes, Malik held her gaze and told her, "Khadijah, you are a beautiful woman, but according to your name, you had no choice but to be." The name Khadijah is Arabic in nature, but before you arrive, I looked it up in Kiswahili. To me, Kiswahili gives us a more African sense of self. As I strove to produce it in the form of our native tongue, I perceived the significance of your name to mean beloved, faith, hope, love, unity and peace. Tell me you weren't created to be beautiful? Just so you can always be in the presence of physical evidence of who you really are, I had the librarian run off and laminate this copy for you to keep."

Getting up to return the book to its shelf, Malik felt pride tugging at his heart. Not quite able to put his finger on it, there laying just beneath the surface, was an ambiguous contrast between the woman he saw and the woman he knew existed. Upon his return, Malik asked Khadijah her favorite food. The true personification of a "sista", fried chicken was her reply. Chicago, being the pentagon of culinary excellence, he had just the place in mind. Watching the sway of her corpulent hips, he allowed Khadijah to lead him out onto Halsted Street, the busiest intersection in the city.

CHAPTER 18

Harold's Chicken was crowded, as usual, but Malik was able to find a nice corner booth that afforded he and Khadijah a fraction of privacy. After placing an order akin to a small feast, Malik hesitated until the waitress was out of hearing range. Taking a deep breath, as he pulled out his personal Quran, he warned the dynamic Misses Dupree that he was indeed attracted to her in a strong way. However, his beliefs deemed that every man of the faith needed to take a Muslimah—female Muslim—on as his wife. With this being said, his aim was to introduce her to the Islamic faith for both spiritual, as well as personal, purposes. Turning to Surah an-Nahl (16):97, he quoted verbatim, "Whoever does a righteous deed, whether male or female, and is a true believer, we will give him a good life (by granting him contentment) and He will reward them in the hereafter in the accordance with the best of what they used to do."

Taking a few seconds to process the Surah, Khadijah reached across the table, grabbed both of Malik's hands, and looked into his eyes. "Maybe you are seeing me through jaded lenses. Sometimes our minds can make us see in a person what they want us to see. Make no mistake, I'm fond of Prince Ali, however, I'm traveling the unused path of spirituality out of attraction. In fact, the whole concept of love, God—in your case Allah—are all foreign entities to me. My life, nevertheless, revolved around either mystery. Malik, I'm a calloused being. All representation of my devotion was erased before I ever took my first breath. Where you inherited spiritual erudition, my knowledge is worldly and more of an ungodly understanding of life. Granted, I'm a woman and hold on to all of the feminine dreams of fairy tales. I yearn to wake up to a family—a husband and kids—in due season, but understand, in order for me to identify with your spiritual manifestations, it's imperative for me to break your words down to the least common denominator, nod, and take a more scientific approach. For example, "Everything in the realm of science revolves around gravity.""

Conversation ceased as the waitress delivered their order to the table. Tasting the chicken, Khadijah subconsciously licked the crumbs from the corner of her lips. In Malik's eyes, the gesture was erotic. Grabbing his order of breast and thighs—dark meat only—he relished the taste of the apple butter oven baked fries. Sliding out of the booth, Khadijah joined Malik on his side of the table. As she slid in, she informed him that her definition of gravity is this—the physical attraction between two material bodies. "So, tell me," she asked between bites, "Mr. Rafsanjani, is love equal to gravity?" Regaining some sense of control, Malik took over the conversation. "Khadijah, I questioned Prince Fazaad Ali as to your occupation, seeing as to how impressive your portfolio seemed to be. Holding you in high esteem and loyal to your confidence, his answer was simply, 'questionable.' I strive in my everyday walk to attain paradise at life's end. My mutual understanding of this is an experience so wonderful as to defy description. But, even so, it's still a mystery yet to be discovered. Truth be told, I see paradise in you, Khadijah, but I must ask, who are you, why are you here, and what is your purpose?" Damn near masticating her fingers, she licked the running apple butter from her fingertips. Wiping her mouth with the napkin, she sipped her drink and attempted an answer. "I'm attempting to find myself every day. Really, I don't have a clue as to who I am, but I think I'm on the road to discovery. For less than honorable reasons, I am here. These reasons I don't understand, because by all logic I shouldn't be. My existence is reactive instead of proactive. According to the laws of nature, rape was the action that produced the reaction equal to or greater than the act, with the return resulting in twins. The short version is that my mother died in a car accident minutes before me and my sister were born. The man who donated his sperm was some random rapist in the jungles of Somalia, who captured my mother during a military operation in Africa and made her his personal prisoner of war. I was adopted and separated from my identical twin at the tender age of one years old. As for the other questions, I don't even understand my presence, which makes it all the more complicated trying to figure out my purpose. Malik, you asked questions and expect answers, but I wonder, can a man of your faith and religious convictions handle the truth? In order to help me achieve my best, the challenge comes with accepting and acknowledging me at my worst. I was born with a black heart. My life is void of love, and has been, even from the initial stages of conception. Placing a finger to her lips, Malik said her name in syllables "Kha-di-jah." Your name is beautiful, and when I measure the title against the subject, I'm enthralled by absolute perfection, at the same time, I'm challenged to sort through the debris and uncover the substance. "Okay, Mr. Poetical Justice, ever since I was old enough to understand its pertinence, I've asked myself the same question daily, 'Who am I'? But one night, the smooth chords of a piano ensemble by Bach has inspired me to search diligently until I find the answers. As you can see, I'm on a mission to define myself, but what I need you to comprehend is the difference in realities. In mine, love itself don't love nobody, and when you are faced head on with this understanding from the first developmental stages of childhood, everything takes on the additive inverse of it's counterparts. Sanity becomes insanity, happiness becomes sadness, aggression turns into violence, and what should be clarity takes on the form of chaos. Instead of love, all one knows is hatred and abuse! If these conditions are still favorable of your attraction, then the next time we meet, it will be on my turf, and on my terms. Give me a call when you are ready to visit Augusta."

CHAPTER 19

"**N**ame your price!" The contractor's voice rose an octave higher as his frustration became apparent. The acoustics of his voice vibrated off the walls and the lack of common sense foreshadowed his sanity. Wheeling around to face Khadijah, his beady eyes reminded her of a reptile as his speech became more controlled and calculated. "You little black bitch, I made you! Since the day I brought your little ungrateful ass from California, I sent you to the best training facilities in the world. Before you turned eighteen, you had seen more places than most of you negro ancestors had in their entire lifetime. This is how you repay me? When you and that snotty-nosed, bastardized sister were just wards of the state, I made sure that both of you had a home where you lacked for nothing. I guess now that your bank account has six-digit zeroes, the true color of the dog that you are has surfaced. Why am I even surprised? Your kind has always been happy with scraps… crabs in a muthafuckin' bucket!"

Under the influence of being betrayed, he realized that death lurked in lonely places, and in his moment of blind rage, he may have very well bought a one-way ticket. In order to enhance his tactics of superiority, he tossed the folder containing both—the details and the deed—to the beach front property in Mission Bay, California, at her feet. Engulfed in a ball of murderous rage, Khadijah held his stare as the message hit home. Her foster father's true feelings and intentions were finally out in the open. It only gave validity to her feelings over the years. Confused by his statements, Khadijah tossed the thought around in her mind. She had always wondered why she and her twin had been separated. Understanding hit home, and she had to get out of there before the bile pushing past her intestines totally liquified her hate, and she prematurely up-chucked the suppressed endearments of evil she felt for the faggot. Before Khadijah even cranked the car, the two contractors were on a conference call. Fatima's curiosity grew with every elevated offer they proposed. Finding it an odd request to kill a woman, she had accepted. Fatima had

no hang ups, after all, she was an equal opportunity killer. This contract appeared too good to be true, however,
she would have to be masterfully connected to cover the
tracks of her proceeds. Unconsciously, life had come full
circle; she had been paid a king's ransom to kill a killer. No
amount of training would prepare her for the road ahead!

After Fatimah had been disconnected, the conversation between the contractors was still in full throttle.
One, asked the other, "Why is it so hard to let go? In my
haste, I put my own foot in my mouth. If looks could kill, I'd
have been dead when she walked out the door. You know
just like I do that the eyes are the windows to one's soul.
These bitches have no soul. Remember, we stole them
when we paid that greedy caseworker, Ms. Klein, to alter
the documents and our qualifications, to ensure the process." "Yes, I do remember. Then, the girls were harmless.
These are not your average brother or sister siblings, these
are twins! Their bond goes deeper than bone, flesh and
blood. They are two halves of a whole. All we have on our
side is time. Maybe they won't recognize each other. Even
in the course that they do, let's hope time has deleted any
remnants of affinity. I can promise you this, If Fatimah ahs
any indication that she's been contracted to kill her twin,

everybody involved better be prayed up, 'cause that is the most ecil and heartless black girl walking the face of the Earth! I know your instincts kicked into overdrive, and in our business, instincts are good to have, but they often-times merely mimic mental distress by way of paranoia."

CHAPTER 20

Almost 200 years after Abraham Lincoln signed the Emancipation Proclamation, Charleston, South Carolina was the last state to still have the original marker of the Slave Market. Somehow, the state, through its symbolism, still reminded blacks that no matter how far the world has come, the centrifugal force of the confederate states would always impart the propaganda of slavery. In contrast to the Confederate flag flying, Charleston's Navy Ship Yard was commissioning *The SSN-797 U.S.S. Barack Obama.* The high tech nuclear submarine was named after the first and only Black president of the United States and, presently being constructed in the dry docks of the covertly operational naval base. I bet the now deceased and longest standing senator in history Strom Thurmond, was flopping like a fish out of fresh water in his grave, just knowing that South Carolina was paying homage to one that the reds fought so hard to keep enslaved.

Admiring and enjoying the rich historical sightings of the downtown area, Khadijah made a mental note to visit on her own time. She now had to set up surveillance on her last and final victim. Showing her military ID at the entrance of the naval station, Khadijah had no clue that she was being tailed. Pulling up into the parking lot of the dry dock, she covered her eyes with the ultraviolet shades and stepped out with the intentions of making at least, visual contact with the dead man walking.

Watching Khadijah through the high powered binoculars, from a distance of seventy-five feet, Fatimah gasped at how close in resemblance they were. Watching how the woman gracefully stalked her prey, her movements seemed all too familiar, as if she could really pinpoint her next step. Punctuality pays off; just as Khadijah followed the sound of the pneumatic tools at work, a loud buzzer went off. This was obviously for the navy men and indicated the end of the work day. Suddenly, as if orchestrated, all the drilling, sanding, and other construction ceased. Anxious to be ending another day, the sailors exited tandemly through the gates. Spotting Senior Chief Jerome

Wade instantly, Khadijah licked her lips at the salient features headed her way. Locking eyes with a modern day Nefertiti, Senior Chief Wade innocuously appraised and inspected the raw beauty of his stalker from a distance.

Flirtatiously posing as the damsel in distress, Khadijah motioned to gain the chief's attention. She noticed as his towering figure got closer, that even sweaty and caked with dust and dirt, he was a handsome man. Too bad he had to die. Cheering her victim on and seeing how the sailor became putty in the killer's hands, Fatimah sang out, "You go girl!" You are good, but what happens when the hunter becomes the hunted? Turning at just the right angle, the glare from Khadijah's necklace caught Fatimah's attention. The single swinging half of the set of dog tags had her drawn to the probability of coincidences. Running through her mental checklist, emotions welled up inside as she stared at the physical composite of herself through the windshield of the car. Not fully believing her fortune, she needed to get a little closer to the dog tag hanging loosely around the woman's neck.

The information had been exchanged, and the black widow had spun her web. Fatimah pulled out of the parking lot and headed back to her hotel.

CHAPTER 21

Pulling over about a quarter of a mile outside of the naval base's gates, Fatimah waited for Senior Chief Wade to pass so that she could pick up his tail. Getting a feel for his environment, she could better orchestrate the outcome. She hoped her intuition was wrong. If she'd been tripping and had a case of mistaken identity, then she would kill two birds with one stone. Impressed with the residential area just south of the Ashley Phosphate, Fatimah realized she had a small problem as the oversized Rottweiler rushed to meet his master as the car pulled into the gate. As the plan took form in her mind, her actions could best be defined as whorish as she intended to fuck man and his best friend. Coming to the end of River's Avenue, the subdivision formed a cul-de-sac, and she proceeded in the direction in which she came. Heading to her hotel to get some rest, Fatimah prepared for an early morning of sunrise surveillance.

Posing as an environmentalist, Fatimah was able to conceal her tracking tactics and also, blend in without protruding like a sore thumb. With just a little bit of an imagination, exits can open up and become entrances for those with other-than-honorable intentions. Standing one porch over, the elderly neighbor seemed to be interested in the conversational questionnaire about the contaminants polluting the drinking water in the residential community. Fatimah's heart rate increased as the shadow of her sparrow exited his home in loose fitting white linen slacks, with a form fitting black raw silk shirt. The jacket to the custom made Tom Ford pant suit casually collapsed over his shoulders. She was, gratefully, distracted by the phone ringing and left the questionnaire to be completed with the promise to return later to retrieve them. Being sure to stay six car lengths behind, she followed Jerome ceremoniously around North Charleston. His car pulled up to the nondescript hotel and Fatimah jested her mock jealousy as Khadijah strutted sensuously to the sleek Cadillac awaiting her arrival. Fatimah beamed in admiration as the killer was all costumed up in a Zac Posen evening gown. All this bitch was missing was a horse, carriage, and a muthafuckin frog— watch out Disney.

The sun was starting to set, and nightfall would be her blanket to put the pooch to sleep. Under the impression that they were out on a date, this gave Fatimah plenty of time to prepare, plan, and perfect the plot. The moon slowly traded places with the sun as she slipped up to the gate, untying the pouch containing a dozen infant diamondback rattlesnakes and dumping them into the grass. She snatched her hands back just in the knick of time as the pugnacious beast came barreling around the house. He sank his fangs into the wire mesh of the fence as she retreated to her vehicle. Fatimah noticed the dog focus his attention to the grassy area all around him. He growled ferociously at the creatures of the night until all that could be heard was the wounded whine of a weakening animal. Falling into the role of her alter ego, she shook her head and laughed as the music played. Somebody should have warned Jerome Wade and his best friend that they were fucking the same girl.

Turning into the parking lot off of Meeshaw Parkway, they could see the North Charleston Performing Arts Center was bursting at the seams to support the future actors and actresses who were performing the culturally diverse play, *from gutta to Gullah*. Being from Valdosta, Georgia, himself, he was honored to volunteer his time to educate the performing arts students on the ways of life and the linguistics of the cultured people along the Georgia Carolina coastline.

The intoxicating bass seemed to tranquilize the mood as the patrons filed in to take their seats at the candlelit tables. Openly admiring Khadijah's youthful beauty, affinities spirits seemed to accost Mr. Wade. Instead of a predator's ill desires, he felt a paternalistic need to protect her. Having built an iron curtain between him and his past, understanding danced in the illumination of his face from her question. "Mr. Wade, during your military tenure, have you ever been shipmates with or come into contact with a Petty Officer Destiny Dupree?" The glaze from years of guilt cast a sheen, giving him the exotic pigmentation of varnished black walnut. Knowing that answers are easiest found in the eyes, Khadijah held his stare. Pulling his wallet from his pants, he opened it up to a picture and handed it across the table. There stood her mother, hugged to a mystery man and a younger and physically immature Jerome Wade dressed in dungarees. It's times like this, in a never ending search for validation, where what you don't know can hurt you. He continued to stare and informed her that were best friends. Paused by the polyphony that began the prelude to the performance, both were thankful for the safety of their thoughts. Following every act of the stellar stage show, Khadijah seemed to appreciate the gallantry of the Gullahs. Meanwhile, Jerome was mentally snatched away by the snap, crackle, and pop of his past. As if he were seeing through three-dimensional shade, he relived the scene of the rape. Hearing the echo of Destiny's screams, then Petty Officer First Class Wade, of the covert Sea, Air and Land Squadron, better known as the Navy SEALS, was captured and cordoned off by a group of savage Somolians. By the time he was rescued, every bone from his pinky to his knee cap had been completely broken. When the remaining four members of the black ops squad, code named, "The Seal Seven," crept up in camouflage and cut the captor's throats, they ignored Petty Officer Dupree's screams.

As the inhuman vibrations of her voice rippled the waters of the Nile river, Chief Sexton and Chief Rosecrans looked into Wade's eyes with conspiratorial glances and said, "We sacrified one to save us all!" Not expecting her to make it, the powers that be underestimated her sheer will to survive, and a hush came over them as they were caught with their hands in the cookie jar. Released from the shadows of the rain forest, guilt swung low like sweet chariots as the Z-boat navigated its way through the perils of aquamarine wild life.

The applause ending the show brought Jerome back to the present, and Khadijah looked one last time at the picture before handing back his wallet. Removing the picture from it's plastic sheathing, he handed her the photo for a keepsake. It was kept there as a reminder of his sin of silence. Once inside the comfort of the car, Wade remembered the revelation that quickly turned to rumor. He didn't think it could actually be true. On the drive, Khadijah was given a quick biography of the trio in the picture. They were in the same company, of course an integrated one, in boot camp. He joked about how feisty Destiny's attitude was back then and detailed how her mother fell in love with his best friend. "The relationship started out as one of codependency. Seaman Bush could never quite grasp the art of folding and stowing his uniforms, and Seaman Recruit Dupree was horrible at spit shining her dress shoes. Bush was from the streets and was naturally at odds against authority, and your mom couldn't get along with any of the women in our company to save her life. Then the funniest thing happened, they made Seaman Bush the company's Master-At-Arms. He became solely responsible for the company; everything, from physical training to marching in formation and singing the cadence, rested on his shoulders. Although far from domesticated, he handled his position with the innate qualities of a leader. I still remember it like it was last week. We were getting ready for a company inspection, and our company commanders were being extremely hard on Bush; that's the first time I saw my man crack under pressure. Me, him, and Destiny were speed buffing the laundry room and dude just snapped. Slinging the buffer into the wall, it was in that moment that your mother became like water to a dehydrated soul. Two hydrogen tons to one part oxygen, Destiny, at that point became Bush's fundamental key to life."

Pulling into the drive way, Khadijah and Jerome were laughing to keep from crying. With a need to help Destiny's replica understand who her mother was, he missed the minute detail that his canine was missing in action! Safely stowed away in the walk-in closet, Fatimah listened in and began to quietly disrobe down to her lace bra and thong panties. Listening to the tales of her mother made her feel strange and out of place, but at least she got a little consolation from hearing the stories. "See these pictures? They are ones taken in boot camp. All throughout her career, Bush pushed her to be great. He's the reason she ever made our SEAL team in the first place. Something your mother told him the night before our graduation inspection from basic training stuck in his heart and unleashed the unseen greatness in that man.

Up until the day that he died, he never let me forget what her words did for him, for the both of us. She said, "Bush, your inner sincerity simply flows outwards and comes across in your communication. From your conversation, you impart the wisdom of preacher, teacher, mentor, and leader. Truthfully, I don't think you've discovered your own authority, and this is reason to cause alarm. You must be careful what tables you dine at, because, sometimes, a personality can poison us. Can't you see that together we are a force that's able to overcome anything, but I need you to uncover your true authority. Only then will your eyes be opened to understand that with authority, comes power!"

Moved by the message, and a guilty conscience being the cathartic of a free flowing confession, Wade turned to Khadijah and told her he was there and how there were "rumors that a tortured soul wasn't all Destiny Dupree brought back across the Trans-Atlantic. "Our team leaders had set Bush up to be convicted of a crime he didn't commit right before we deployed for the operation. It was a horrible experience—both me and Destiny were captured. They broke every bone from my toes to my knees before I was rescued. Even under excruciating pain, your mom's melee made me feel less of a man. Our motto is, never leave a man, dead or alive, on the battle field. I felt I should have done more, but physically I was left incapable. Overwrought with despair, Khadijah rushed to the restroom; she had obligations to fulfill, but under these conditions she didn't know if he could kill her mother's only surviving friend.

Creeping up from behind, Fatimah knew her costume would add just a little bit of pleasure on his plunge to death. Stepping up next to Jerome, from both the port and starboard sides, Khadijah stared at her other self in amazement. The hissing sounds seemed deafening in the quiet. Stepping from the shadows, somehow snakes have a way of invoking fear, and the stench of Mr. Wade's vacuous perspiration became unbearable. The afterglow of devilish maternal inheritance reminded him of the lessons of Greek mythology and matriarchal deification. "I've seen you before," Jerome mechanically stated, "those wicked eyes . . . you are the evil apparition of Africa, the motherland, the isolated lot of the beautiful and the bountiful. You're the bi-product of every hardship from famine to fever. What one would call the ultimate African anomaly. How could something so brilliantly beautiful be so esoterically evil?"

He kept his eyes on her body, and Fatimah pushed his mouth closed. She told him, "Although I cycle the same, I am the dark side of the moon, and if art is an imitation of life, then your expression must be a masterpiece. On behalf of me and my twin, we thank you for the shared memories of our mom." Stroking and soothing the serpent, movement activated the jaws of life and the snake struck. methodically sinking its fangs into Jerome Wade's eye socket. As a gift for his information, Fatima's serrated black blade created a line, as it jaggedly sliced his throat!

CHAPTER 22

World renown psychologist, Dr. Jazmine Winters, who was now the president of Southern California's Chapter of Black Psychologists, was both awed and elated to hear from her young charges. With memory replaying itself, she sadly recollected the injustice done to these young ladies years ago at the hands of the California Child Protective Services. Smiling, she wrote the directions down to Khadijah's Mission Beach property, and assured the twins that she would handle the arrangements of contacting their legal representative, Mr. Charlie M. Peutz.

Years after their adoption, Attorney Peutz and Ms. Winters combined their services and now shared a very lucrative working relationship. Neither knowing what happened to the Dupree girls after the separation, they both maintained a macrocosm of meticulously orchestrated financial records. Knowing that one day, they would be contacted to produce bank statements and receipts, they held out hope that the girls had been properly taken care of and often openly discussed the children's welfare. Judging by statistics, the likelihood of Fatimah and Khadijah's mental stability was not favorable. Even though the twins sounded well, Ms. Winters was sure that there had been years of adjustments, maladjustments, and readjustments psychologically, that assisted in their emotional survival.

Picking up on the second ring, Charlie M. Peutz Esquire answered in his usually chipper voice. Basking in the glow of excitement, he listened carefully to his business partner and best friend. Checking his calendar, he assured Jaz, as he affectionately called her, that he would be ready to have lunch on Mission Beach with her and the girls tomorrow. Gathering all the data that applied to the Duprees, Mr. Peutz performed a mental checklist and dreading the end of a tedious but valued pecuniary stipend relationship. Nicknamed, The Ghost Lawyer, Charlie Peutz made most of his wealth lingering in the shadows of his clients. Hanging up with Jaz, he called the Navy Federal Credit Union and advised them that his two clients would need to meet with the branch manager to discuss their financial options and make the proper arrangements.

Bringing each up to par on the progression of their lives, they tender footedly tip-toed around certain subjects that were sure to surface. Slicing through the thick tension, Khadijah handed her sister a printout of the Kiswahili meaning of her name, that Malik had given her as a reminder of her worth and carefully spied her reaction as she read the contents. Upon registered understanding, emotions broke like the Water Gate Scandal. Anger showed through the tense twitching of Fatimah's jaw line and revelation filled her mind like biblical prophesy. Looking starry-eyed at her twin, she said, "They knew it didn't they?" Clueless, Khadijah wanted and waited for her to continue. "They knew that as long as they could keep us from our self-identity, that they could raise us up to be puppets and have control of the strings. Don't you get it? They kept us separated knowing that we'd be incomplete, because we are two halves of one whole. Together we could have figured it out and found our own way, but as long as we were divided, they could control and manipulate our complimentary characteristics. From birth, we operated on a single set of beliefs and desires, the obsession of one becoming the obsession of the other. Mix these properties with the obsequious qualities of childhood. I recall, for as long as I can remember, waking up at odd hours, having pains run through my body for no apparent reason, even catching colds out of the blue. I never lost sight that we were synchronized and were two bodies operating off one mind. To know the mind of one was to know the mind of us both, because our disciplines and objectives were the same. Do you believe in mind projection? Our natural hate for service men was innate. It's hard to put the pieces together because we have yet to sort through Destiny's repository, but I'm willing to bet that the missing pieces are there!" Khadijah had one more thing stirring the troubled waters of her mind. "How did you find me after all this time?" Averting her sister's eyes, she explained that she was paid to find her. Tossing the folder in her lap, Fatimah forcefully told her, "You were under contract."

CHAPTER 23

Pulling up in the Royal Purple sleek Audi RS-5, Jazmine Winters, personifying the epitome of professionalism, kicked off her Chanel jeweled sandals. Leaving her footprints in the sand, her egg shell White Victoria Becham linen dress flapped around her toned calves as she made her way to the beach house. Uplifted by the thoughts that at least one of the Dupree sisters was doing good for herself, Ms. Winters stopped at the stand just west of Khadijah's steps and ordered a Pina Colada slushy. WIth her signature designer shades covering her eyes, Jaz slipped on her sandals and strutted up the winding stairs.

Excited and anxious, Fatimah and Khadijah rushed through the door to greet the only maternal example they had ever trusted. Holding each other's arms, uprooted by their physical beauty, Jaz realized that she couldn't tell them apart. Nonetheless, the moment was emotionally charged, and she was happy to see that the system hadn't been successful at breaking their spirits. Both sisters withdrew at the possibility that Ms. Winters would inquire about background information. Adopting her sensory skills under the tutelage of Dr. Na'im Akbar, she caught the sudden shift of wariness. She would only take what the twins were willing to give. Diffusing the emotionally charged encounter, the ringing of the bell saved them all the awkwardness of embarrassment. Not as connected, but just as defendant and grateful to the now super successful lawyer, Charlie M. Peutz. Khadijah and Fatimah group hugged him into their embrace. Telling them that they had a lot of ground to cover this morning, they felt the surreal reality that the past was their only hope of having a functional future. Ignorant to the intensity of this reunion, Mr. Peutz was whistling to his own tune. Parading the streets of San Diego in the company of three of the most beautiful woman this side of the 405 freeway would make him the obsession and envy of every white man with jungle fever. And in the melting pot of the "Gold Coast", interracial relations was the norm.

Wondering what the gathering crowd of beach goers was all about, Fatimah and Khadijah enjoyed being the center of attention as Mr. Peutz held the door of the super stretched limousine. Flashing million dollar smiles at the many lust filled stares, they all disappeared behind the tinted windows, lounging in the lap of luxury. Not knowing what to expect after all these years, their lawyer felt that it was the least that he could do. In no way did it make up for the decision of the Child Protection Agency, but it was his way of separating himself from the cruel and unjust system. Once seated in the soft leather seats, he handed Fatimah and Khadijah each their own financial portfolios. The accounts that they had never touched, grew by almost double over the years. Although, both were overcompensated for financially, it was nice to know that someone took their interests seriously. After being formally introduced to the Chief Operating Officer of the Navy Federal Credit Union, they were lead to the facility's repository, where Destiny's most intimate artifacts had been kept under lock and key for almost twenty years. Everything was neatly packed into two carry along footlockers. As each sister grabbed a locker, they were then lead to the financial office where they had decisions to make and forms to complete.

"As the supervising entity of this facility, it is my pleasure to finally welcome you ladies. Mr. Peutz and I have met semi-annually since my tenure began, therefore all statements are current. At this time, I would ask you to consider accepting our preferred customer package. Included in this package is our life and medical, as well as automobile and dental insurance that I feel is second-to-none. Your current 6% annual interest rates will move up over a point, making it 7.5%, with free unlimited checking options and access to our federally funded and insured debit and platinum credit cards. Both of you are pre-approved for car, business, and home loans up to the extent of your current account balances. Last but not least, as long as you reserve your rights to our membership, your military ID's are good on an inactive status. Now, I'll leave you ladies to confer with your attorney. If you agree, then it's as simple as the touch of a button, but if you choose otherwise, I'll print Cashier's Checks for the both of you, then you can be on your way."

They advised both Fatimah and Khadijah that they couldn't find any better banking incentives in the civilian world, and they would be crazy to decline this opportunity. Accepting the advice, and as if on cue, the COO returned with checks printed and a stack of deposit and withdrawal slips. He handed each twin their personal NFCC banking cards, which he explained could be used like a credit card without the usage fees. Before exiting, Khadijah asked him to explain their banking transfer procedures, and step-by-step he filled an example copy of the form for her to keep and handed them instruction paperwork with their banking and routing numbers to seal the deal. They were given keys to individual safety deposit boxes that had been prepaid for a year.

Tired from the events of the day, Khadijah and Fatimah closed their eyes on the ride back to the beach, each mentally preparing for what lie ahead in Destiny's annals, which had been concealed up until now. Even though the system separated them just as their personalities began to emerge, it would be the wisdom and suffering of a mother that they had never known that would nourish the buds to blossom.

CHAPTER 24

Under the influence of a good night's sleep, the twins joined each other on the wraparound veranda and let the salt riding the air from the ocean tenderize their flawless skin. Googley eyed, they popped the lock to one of their mother's chests. Placing the trunk between them, item by item, they carefully studied the material. Starting with Destiny's boot camp picture book, Fatimah, the more eagle eyed of the duo, gasped as she studied the class picture. The twins learned that their mother went to basic training in Orlando, Florida, where there seemed to be men and women in the picture. This was known in the Navy as an integrated company. After spotting Destiny, Khadijah was ready to flip the pages. Grabbing her sister's hand, she asked her if she recognized anything strange. Shaking her head in the negative, Fatimah began to read off the names. "Maybe just a coincidence." They continued turning the pages. About mid-way through the book, there was a picture depicting seven crisp and creased Navy Seamen. Six males and one female had been chosen to try out for the Special Forces branch of the Navy upon graduation from their A-Schools. Seaman Recruits Destiny Dupree, Cedric Vinson, and Jerome Wade; Seaman Apprentices Randy Cox and Robert Robblier; And Seaman Benson Leopoldo and Cleveland Bush.

Analytical minds kicking into overdrive, they just stared at each other as the information Jerome Wade had given them before he died became buttressed by the evidence. According to Wade's final testimony, everybody in this photo is dead, including Seaman Bush, who was supposed to have been dating their mother and was thought to have been set up for a crime he didn't commit because he protected Destiny's rights to become the first Black female Navy Seal. Also, suffering from diarrhea of the larynx, Mr. Wade explained that Seaman Cleveland Bush was killed in a riot at the military prison in Leavenworth Kansas, and that our adopted fathers were the commanding officers of the special and clandestine operations where Destiny was purposely left for dead in Somalia.

From birth, neither twin harbored any spontaneous urges to shed a tear. But, here they were, reunited under less than honorable conditions, facing the harsh cold reality. Finally, the warmth of familial validation had created the heart of belonging. Coming across a travelogue of their military experience together, the twins laughed and cried at picture after picture, taken in various places.

Destiny and Seaman Bush seemed happy and photogenic together. Khadijah C.S.I.'d the picture and said to the image reflected back to her, "So this is what love looks like, huh?" Coming out of her trance, Khadijah witnessed the sporadic convulsions of her sister and relieved her of what appeared to be a letter, knowing this must be the handwriting of Seaman Bush, posthumously speaking to her soul. Hesitantly, she spied the neat penmanship and began to read the letter aloud:

MAY 13,2010

Greetings Destiny,

It is with the hopes that love, blessings and peace console you. Officially I'm counting down—not the days to my release but the days to my freedom. I got a date, although not with you, it's still a date to my destiny, none-the-less. Rose-crans and Sexton have blackballed me, and every tomorrow that I see will be no differnt than today. I'm haunted by the hateful and evil stares of the military police that guard me. Already I'm dead because they've killed my character. Now I just wish they would open their hands and let me spit my last breath in the palms of their hands. I've suffered the harshest torture tactics that they cab give and, just as you did, when you passed the SEAL exam, smile in the faces of their weak rendition of masculinity. With authority comes power, so they threw ne ibn this cage to contain ny superiority. By the tine this letter reaches you, I hope to have journeyed to my transition in the hereafter. After all, Destiny, this ain't about me, it's about truth. See, in truth, to uplift the woman is to uplift the world.

You should know that you can't rise up any consciousness in others if your own consciousness is not yet risen. How can you teach others self love, if you don't love and respect your-self? Destiny, I've always pushed you hard, 'cause a nation can rise no higher than it's women. You symbolize the har-vest and fertility of the Earth. You are the foundation of black soil, which the sheer essence of life will grow. To acknowledge creation as a whole, obne simply must acknowledge the *components through which it was, and is being, fashioned. The science of creation reveals that women are the cradle and cornertone to ay true form of civilization. As a women, you are naturally a vessel of God, you've bee ordained with the resources to facilitate the process of creation.*

Know that the trickery of female subjugation is a spawn of social and psychological insecurity; and understand that whatever mental state you are in, development quite naturally will follow. I heard about the operation. I probably know more about it than you do, but trust me, karma travels in all directions. The unjust will get their due! Love is love! A man that is born into slavery can, at best, die a slave, only then, can he attain true freedom.

To you I impart love, life, and loyalty.

—CLEVE

Unable to plunge any deeper, Fatimah retreated within herself. Stomped by the emotional vicissitudes, Khadijah stumbled upon the official documents stamped Naval Department of Psychiatry. She wondered just how badly the ordeal in Africa affected her mother. Hopping the hurdle of healing, the ballast tank began to open up and fill her spirit with the understanding of absent emotions. The entry read as such:

I want to again enjoy the psychological benefits of love. No matter how demeaning and traumatic the experience was, with the help of an unnamed human clone of an animal, I hope to create a new individual, a personality, a soul. My far off fantasies of family were nebulous at best. Even though the experience shattered my spirit, within me, my soul began to re-crystallize itself. Despite all ethical, religious, and logical questions and concerns, I'm keeping these babies dirty diapers and all! I thrive for the day, where again, I would have someone to care for, someone who requires and reciprocates my love. At least with twins, if something were to ever force my babies into the same loveless position as me, at least they can crawl under the cloak of each other's affection.

As the deep dark void began to suck sentimentality straight from the bowels of these cold-hearted killers, they desperately needed a diversion. The urge to be in Malik's company manifested itself in the form of a migraine headache and Malik was the medicine. Tossing everything back inside the trunk, Khadijah grabbed Fatimah by her arm, and they went inside. Dialing the 312 area code, Khadijah was hopeful he had someone to pair her sister off with. Reaching the answering service, Khadijah left a message. A salaamu aleikum, this has been a trying week, and I'm in need of your company. I'm in San Diego with my sister, and we both just need to get away.

I know this is on short notice, but if there is someone you could pair Fatimah up with, I would be grateful. Malik, she's not as open as I am, I must warn you. I look forward to hearing from and seeing you son. Inshaallah. Call me back at (619) 377-1347.

CHAPTER 25

Deception, trickery, hate, and death was the soundtrack to Fatimah and Khadijah's lives. They were sisters, pulled apart then reunited by destiny, luck, or a higher power. Both sisters wondered would the bond be stronger, and would the anger run deeper the second time around? Life is a bitch with a malicious sense of humor, but the universal law of gravity clearly states: What goes up must come down, and what goes around will eventually come back around again. The children who suffer today will be the men and women who inflict suffering tomorrow. The intense pain of feeling raw and scraped internally began to subside, and the shock of self serving sympathy started to fade.

By the end of their undercover reunion, secrets had been revealed, and the twins were on a mission to rebuild the moral and spiritual foundation of their beings. Now, the only piece of the puzzle that was missing, revenge, is being carefully plotted. The cure for hate at times is more deadly than the cause and in this case served as a necessary evil to create order out of chaos. Fatima and Khadijah Dupree had symbolized the mythical phoenix to a militarist male chauvinistic conspiracy theory. The desired affect was, for the girls to rise up out of the ashes, and explode, in turn incinerating all evidence of the traumatizing treatment of the only female that tamed the testosterone of the male dominated secret sect. The jingle of the palm sized iPhone startled them. Motioning for Khadijah to be quiet, Fatimah pressed the speaker phone button. Not one to waste words, the contractor explained that he had just gotten confirmation of a Senior Chief Jerome Wade's execution in Charleston, South Carolina. Today, he purchased a fully functional recording studio in Lake Charles, Louisiana, and as they speak it was being overhauled with all of the state of the art equipment. Then, he stated that Sexton had tossed in a "fresh off the showroom floor" Mercedes Benz SL-550 Convertible. "There were only one hundred made of this class. Fatimah, the man is paranoid and hoping for your expedient attention. The sooner we can meet for the final inspection of you Lake Charles Property, the sooner Sexton's problem can become a faded memory. Here's the address, and if you happen to beat me in, there's a stone gargoyle statue on the porch; the keys are tucked away in the ass."

Seeing her sister shaking in anger, Fatimah hugged her and said, "It's almost over. They played right into my hands. Let's enjoy our weekend and Sunday night we'll drive out to Lake Charles. Don't think Louisiana is ready for Hurricane Khadijah!" The shrill ringing of the landline phone created a welcomed diversion from the already forming visions in their minds. Inspecting the caller ID, Khadijah snatched it up thinking it must be Dr. Winters; who else would it be calling her from a San Diego area code? Upon answering, she was met by the Islamic greeting, and she returned it. Gasping at how much her sister resembled their mom when she smiled, Fatimah realized that only one thing could produce a facial expression that radiant, and figured it must be the infamous Malik. Cheesing like a Cheshire cat, Khadijah was in utopia, an imaginary place where life is perfect and everyone is happy. Hanging up the phone, she ran around getting dressed in a hurry. Finally flawless, in a cool and sexy Twenty8Twelve jersey dress and a pair of flat Rene' Caovilla sandals, she told Fatimah to get dressed because they were having company. Not down for being a third wheel, Fatimah figured she'd dress to impress and maybe after meeting this life changing man, she would grace one of the clubs on the beach with her presence. Finally, life didn't seem so claustrophobic, and soon she could live the life that her mother had intended for them to have.

Stepping out of the tub, Fatimah decided to treat herself to a lemon sugar facial scrub. She mixed one table spoon of brown sugar, one teaspoon of almond oil, and a few drops of juice from a lemon. Massaging the mixture until it was soaked into her face, using slow circular motions, she could feel her skin tightening and rinsed with warm water. Feeling refreshed and restored, she began to pull on the Tracey Reese minidress accented by a pair of Jimmy Choo suede open toe sandals to complete the look. Elegantly simple, the only piece of jewelry she wore was her half of the dog tags she shared with Khadijah.

Beauty stands alone; she needed no additives or preservatives. Looking herself over in the mirror, she felt a little overdressed to be playing tag along. Hearing the front door shut, she sprayed just a touch of Pink on the inside of her wrists and rubbed it in.

Fatimah's heart sputtered as she rounded the corner to see two mid-twenty something model type brothas staring back at her. Standing to greet her, the darker complexioned of the two, held out a hand and said, "Let me guess… You must be Fatimah?" Returning his firm handshake, she said, "You must be Malik?" Coming to stand beside the other man in the room, he introduced everyone to his best friend, Alfred Adams Jr. Using every ounce of her peripheral vision, and without averting her eyes once, she took in every detail. Shaking her hand and holding it a little to long, Alfred said, "My friends call me "Sha-Born," and, as of this moment, I would like to think that we can become friends."

Returning to demagnetize the moment, Malik also had another surprise for them both. Shaking his head, dizzy from nothing but pure beauty, Sha handed each sister a case with three autographed copies of his books, including his latest novel *Players*. Hyperventilating and almost passing out, Khadijah was elated to meet her favorite urban author in physical form. Not as into urban literature as her twin, Fatimah exuded a phlegmatic character, but was just as equally impressed by Mr. Adams. With pictorial evidence of belonging, Khadijah wanted to involve Malik into her family life and offered the montage of her mother. Although lighter in skin tone and a tad bit shorter, the three clearly could have passed for triplets. Asking for a private space to perform Salaat, Khadijah showed Malik to her bedroom and watched to learn the rituals of the prayer.

Taking his chance, Sha-Born told Fatimah that although her beauty was beyond physical comprehension, her eyes seemed somewhat empty. Only an emptiness so completely void can come from one not knowing themselves. Aspiring that, due to the fact that she is the Original Woman, only the consecrated of the Original Man has the insight that something was lacking. "Fatimah, as the Original Woman, you have thirteen genes called mitochondria, and only females possess this special set of genes located inside of their egg cells. They are used as tracing tools because they remain intact, unmixed, and unchanged through generations." Douglass Wallace, a genetic scientist from Emory University was able to test these genes from samples worldwide. Tests results showed two patterns ... both being traced to either Asia or Africa—thus making women of color, specifically Black women, mothers of ancient civilization. I know there is a lot of pain stored inside that comes from the lack of knowledge of self. How do I know? Because as you learn who you are, the world could never disrupt that awesome smile!"

Grabbing Fatimah by the hand, they walked outside, right up to the beaches shoreline, kicked off their shoes and started to walk. *If you have never seen the sunset beyond the horizon to the ocean, you don't know what life is really about*, Fatimah thought. Casting an orange glow way out over the water, their movement stopped, and wiping away the traces of her tears, he motioned for her to look. "I need you to think deep about this next question. As you look at the Earth from this angle, do you notice any resemblance to yourself?" Creeping up on their rear, Malik and Khadijah joined them. Not fluently forming an answer, Sha lifted Fatimah's chin to look into her eyes and continued to teach. "The Earth is three-fourths water and so are you. Malik asked me here because he knew that once you and Khadijah were reunited, there would be a volcano of untended emotions waiting to erupt, and out of loyalty and friendship, I wanted to attempt to offset the tremors. I came for you, but I am the one who's honored. I believe the more that I get to know you, the more that I'll be the one to benefit from our meeting. Khadijah and Fatimah, as you heal, please accept these three steps to serenity. A lot has happened this week, and in order to comprehend the meaning, there are three rules you must follow: Deconstruct your demons, stay in the moment, and find your spiritual balance."

CHAPTER 26

Blissfully unaware of the tragedy closing in around them, retired Admirals Sexton and Rosecrans took the Lake Charles exit off of I-10 and punched the address into the navigation system. In deep thought, Sexton shocked his compatriot with a name, one neither of them had spoken in many of years. "All of this because that bitch, Destiny Dupree, didn't want to stay in a woman's place, just had to walk around holding her nuts! How she ever made it out of Africa alive is beyond me, but after all, it's her homeland. I still remember it like it was yesterday; it wasn't that long ago when women had no rights at all … fix my food and fuck! What has this world come to? First I had to bow down to that Black bitch, and if that wasn't enough, now I have to bow down to her bastards. To hell with a woman and her rights. When that happened Uncle Sam became

my aunt. The idea to set Seaman Bush up was pure ge-
nius; Rosy thought that would sit her ass down, but she
just had to catch us in the act didn't she? A lot of good
men had to die to keep our secret safe, but that's just the
way of the world, I guess. The automated system advised
the driver to take the next right on Moeling Street, travel
half a block down and the destination address would be
on the right. Shutting the engine off on the Porsche 911,
Sexton informed his partner that he had a good mind to
take his service revolver and kill both of the bitches himself. Laughing at his partner's false bravado, Rosecrans
opened his door, looked at Sexton, and said, "That wom-
ens inferiority shit is a thing of the past. You got a complex and you better get over it; these women are trained
killers!" Ascending the stairs, Sexton whispered "Assassins
don't scare me." Tilting his head at the quartz blue Benz,
he said, "I got 550 reasons to say you are lying."

Taking their seats at the wet bar, Fatimah retrieved a
pot of "every white man's poison. Freshly brewed beans,
imported straight from the fields of Castro Country, and
a China dish full of Jamaica's principle export was an
aroma to activate the most dehydrated person's saliva
glands. Playing the perfect host, she poured them each

a cup and gestured to the sugar bowl, advising them to pour their own poison. After pumping three teaspoons a piece into their cups, Fatimah winked her eye, sipped her Java and told them, "I take my coffee just like I take my man—strong, black, and straight!" Flexing her superior technological knowledge, she sashayed to the console of the huge mixing board, balanced out the controls on the equalizer, and looped the sample of James Brown's song, The Big Payback. The music's baseline bounced off the soundproof walls.

Once their cups of coffee had been downed, Fatimah was given the title to the Benz and deed to the studio. Both being blank for her to sign, Rosecrans gave her the information needed to solidify ownership. Noticing the sluggishness begin to settle in, she assured them that she was satisfied with her compensation and the job would be completed expediently. Boosting her ego, Sexton said, "That's why I chose you; I know you are the best." They stood and dropped to the floor as if they had been gutted and filleted. Fatima reminded them that she was only half of the best, and with both men passed out, she facetiously said, "I don't think y'all can stand the whole thing!"

CHAPTER 27

Eight thousand milligrams of finely granulated Seroquel, mixed with pure cane sugar, in this case, a superman's kryptonite, provided enough sedative to tranquilize a fully grown gorilla. Still in a sleep induced haze of fog, and suffering from the dehydration of the Seroquel, both men were handcuffed perpendicularly to props welded from the floor and the ceiling. Eyes focused on the twins, it was obvious that time hadn't played out as they had predicted. "Tell me, Rosecrans, was it all about protecting the fraternal order, or was M.O.M., (Military Order of Masons) just a costume to conceal your true nature and desires? I guess your goat ride was addictive, huh? Heard you passed up a scholarship in baseball to be a soldier. What was your position, did you pitch or did you catch? You left Destiny Dupree, your shipmate, your soldier-at-arms, and your fellow citizen, for dead to keep your secrets from creeping out of the casket. Silence and secrecy—a deadly combination—classified conspiracy theories that depend on the ability of soldiers to keep their mouths shut. You had confidence in the paucity of your ranks because you could easily 'patch up the leaks'. Is that why you set up Seaman Bush? Then when the reigns got too slick for you to control, your only option was damage control!"

Fear has the tendency to make a weak man desperate. Can you smell it, Khadijah? It's all in the air around us, the intimidation of what we may, or may not, know. Sexton, the human parrot, good ol' Rosecran's yes-man. "Tell me, did you have the balls or were you the bitch?" "Naw Khadijah, I think Sexton liked to catch. Uncle Sam saved a whole lot of freaks with his 'don't ask, don't tell' policy, but then again, white male dominance has always been tied to indefinite dual sexuality. To keep the moral identity of the elite class intact was the sole purpose of the policy in the first place. Sexism, classism, and racism—the three ingredients that perpetuate world domination has been strangled by its own chauvinistic hands. Hell Week time, gentlemen. Each hour that you are alive will mentally represent one day of the most physically challenging weeks of your lives. The clock starts now! Khadijah, the show is yours." Pulling up a lawn chair, Fatimah sat back and watched as if it were the greatest show on Earth.

Pushing her portable participant to the far left of the men, Khadijah turned on the strobe lights and pushed play on the receiver. The man named in honor of the last Inca Chief to be tortured, brutalized and murdered by the Spanish Conquistadors rapped "Hail Mary" from his album *The 7-Day Theory*. Changing emotional colors like a chameleon, her mood fluctuated between subtle and psychotic. Khadijah snatched their blindfolds off. Rosecrans and Sexton looked back and forth between the twins, and their skin tones turned the color of spoiled milk as the defeat became evident in their eyes. Enjoying the entertainment, Fatimah removed herself from the chair and stood beside her twin. The silhouette of the sisters enhanced the terror; reduced to merely shadows, the twins exuded a force ten times their actual size, and gauging each other's need for redemptive revenge, mentally, they began to coordinate their points of reference to previously enacted deeds of hellacious evil.

Desensitized, Khadijah nodded in the direction immediately to the men's left. She snatched the shield from the veiled and naked female. "Caseworker Klein, how nice of you to join us. I believe the last time we met, the end resulted in me and my twins separation. But, don't worry, I give you my word, Mr. Rosecrans and Mr. Sexton will forever keep you company! Look at the three of you, strapped helplessly in the pentagram position. Both of you are traveling men, don't look so surprised to see old Gloria Klein. After all, she is your eastern star. Tell me if I'm right.It is your belief that knowledge arises in the East, isn't it? Damn, it's your doctrine that makes the world go round, and just like you, I travel from East to West." Laughing, she continued, "Eve tricked your stupid asses again." Digging into the two separately woven baskets, each sister held up a rotten apple. Stepping directly in front of the men, they held them to their noses so they could both smell the wretched stench of decay. Ad-libbing, Fatimah said to them, it only take one to spoil the whole bunch, and as if motivated by some unforeseen cue, the twins roared back like World Series pitchers, zooming the rotten apples straight into the areas that makes them men. Screaming out in horrendous pain, Khadijah and Fatimah slapped each other high fives and told them they didn't need them anyway.

Resembling the devil and her handmaiden, one of the

twins looked back and said, "Y'all think Gloria Klein got y'all fucked up? Wait until I show you the real strength of the serpent! Just relax. We still have plenty of time, so enjoy the show."

Repositioning the concocted portable contraption that held Mrs. Klein captive, just inches in front of Rosecrans and Sexton, the twins stepped on each side of the woman. On cue, each counted a predetermined number of hair strands and held them gently in their hands. Khadijah whispered in her ear, "They say the love of money is the root of all evil. If this is true then me and my sister must be the fruit of a very demonic flower." Yanking the clusters of hair from her head, leaving instant patches and bald spots, Gloria howled out in excruciating pain. Then strand by lightly bleached blond strand, they plucked until she resembled nothing more than a white girl with a bad weave. With their eyes closed as if her screams were saturating their souls, Fatimah pulled a hand held whip made of nine knotted cords fixed into a handle from her endless bag of tricks. Without feeling or remorse, she slapped the whip right across the bridge of the two men's noses. This pulled them from their pusillanimous retreat, and as if scolding an indolent child about not doing their work in class, she reminded them of how rude their behavior was.

If there was any truth to the theory that hysteria requires energy, then Khadijah Dupree was running off of batteries. Refreshed by her personal pain, the demons finally broke free and became visible. All cried out and numb to the pain, Gloria Klein little more than grimaced at the sight of the razor sharp scimitar. In a slow and animated motion, Khadijah started carefully carving the layers of skin from her face. Peeking past Fatimah's shoulders defiantly, Sexton and Rosecrans became nauseous at the reflection of their fate. Taking a glance and admiring her other half's handiwork, she spoke to the men. "That looks like it really hurts, but at this stage, pain is life!"

CHAPTER 28

How far would you have gone to hide your homosexuality? I have to give credit to the "Father of Psychology", Sigmund Freud, for giving definition to sick bastards like you! Pausing to look at the time, Fatimah held her watch up and called her sister's name. Without hesitation, and in fluid motion as if it were second nature, Khadijah grabbed a fist full of what was left of Case-Worker Klein's hair and cut her head clean off of her shoulders. Disgorging their guts, Sexton began to urinate down his scrawny legs. Tossing Mrs. Klein's severed head into his chest, leaving blood smeared on his skin. Bitch slapping him,

Khadijah hawk spat in his face…So, you want this ungrateful black bitch dead, huh? Swinging the whip and with every lash it opened up skin. Pouring blood as if in ceremonial libation, Khadijah said, I betcha Willie Lynch didn't plan for the shoe to be on the other foot when he gave his famous speech on the bank of the James River, Christmas Eve in 1712. Catching her sister's arm, Fatimah made reference to the time and told her…Not yet! Squatting down beside the decapitated head, Fatimahlaughed demonically at the sickly Ochre colored liquid draining from the hair, and as if just passing around girl talk, she said Mrs Klein, you devil, you—you never told me you were into golden showers!"

Standing to her feet, she counted her fingers as she called off the titles; Absolute Invert, Homosexual, Faggot, Fuck-Boy or just plain old Booty Bandits. Sensing the emotional charge oozing from Rosecrans for the first time as he exerted angry energy against his restraints. While she was walking away, she said…"it's good to enjoy every little perk of life while you can. Don't take your next breath for granted! "

Returning with a small duffle bag, Fatimah tossed it at the men's feet. Either their minds were playing tricks on them, or the bag was actually moving! Keeping a close eye on the bag, he never seen it coming as she grabbed Rosecran's face by his jaws. Tilting his head to look into her eyes. She said it, snapping her other fingers, control; "absolute power causes absolute corruption". Since treason can only be caused by those you trust, when you get to Hell, tell Jerome Wade 'hello' for me. The charges against you are sexual corruption, it's just too bad for you that me and my twin happen to be both, the judge and the jury. Guilty as charged!"

Tell me Rosecrans, back in the Jungles of Africa, did you think when you left Destiny to die that "White Right" would fertilize "Black Fight"? The government has turned a blind eye to its racist in uniform too long. Even the Klan don't recognize the double propaganda that they push. They denounce interracial relations and homosexuality and calls for a secure future for their so-called "white, pure, christian children." I guess they never took into account the White Pure Christian Priests who molest these children and make mockery of the laws of heterosexuality. Some of the same faces that hide under the cloak of the white sheet have been victimized by the same vicious cycle, and it's scientifically as well as statistically proven that children who get abused before breakfast will be guilty of abuse by dinner.

Driven by Black Emotions, Fatimah's form took on a vile glow as she handled the poisonous snake with ease.

In the still and silent embodiment of contained danger, the room went deathly quiet as all eyes were fixated on the serpent. Wrapping the 3ft Rattler around Sexton's neck, she warned him to be very still cause at the first sign of nervous energy the snake would strike in self defense. Hissing and it's tail producing a low rattle, in the fit of petrified rage, Rosecrans made a pitiful attempt to wrestle himself free from the binds. Unaware of the rearing of the snake's head and the elevated vibrations of the rattling, in a lightening quick strike, the reptile's fangs embedded themselves into Rosecran's temple.

Pumping the deadly venom into his bloodstream, it choked off the oxygen from getting to the brain and Mr. Rosecrans experienced a particularly painful 10-15 second shutdown as the brain depleted its 10 seconds of worth of stored oxygen, and his existence came to an untimely end. Watching his friend's body go limp, Fatimah pouted and told Sexton, it's no fun when one dies prematurely … guess he really was the bitch! Noticing how much time had passed by, she said damn, "it's funny how time flies when we are having so much fun". Only 15 minutes left until the tick of the 7th hour. Reaching for the smaller duffel bag, she wanted over to Sexton's exposed ear and whispered, "Have you ever been serenaded by scorpions?" Holding the bag open for the visual inspection, she started to explain, "What we have here is a mixture of extremely dangerous red scorpion, non-poisonous Whip Scorps. Whips are carnivorous and nocturnal. Meaning they eat flesh and hunt in the dark. Wish there were more time for foreplay, at last when you get to hell you can tell them you were the last man standing!" Unzipping the small duffel, Fatimah pulled it open by the straps and shoved the bag over Sexton's head. Holding the mouth of the duffle snug around his neck, she could feel his body jerk with every strike of the Scorpions. Sensing her sisters own fear, Fatimah told her to twist open the valves on the acetylene bottles and the gas formed a mist over the room. Slipping her half of the dog tag from around her neck, she placed it over Khadijah's head. My sister, this symbolizes completion. Placing the keys to the Benz and the blaming title into her hand, Fatimah then told her that She left her instructions and access to everything at the Beach House in Mission Bay. Eyes tears, she informed Khadijah, they were the polarity of opposites. "Where you are the light, I am the dark, where you strive to be right…I have a fascination with doing wrong; where, morally you've embraced growth-I represent spiritual deterioration… and where you choose life, I am ready to meet death. It's the Universal Law of Duality, we needed each other to be able to understand our predestined outcome". Coughing from the gas, Fatimah explained…. Once I light this match, the acetylene gas will mix with the oxygen in the it and burn at 1700 degrees. That's the required temperature to completely incinerate a human body. The only way they'll be able to identify any of us is through dental records, but don't worry, I've never been to the dentist. Smiling, she said now get out of here and find Malik and continue our legacy. "If there's truly a thing called love, then through this deed it's what I leave to you".

Calling her sisters name as the flames grew higher and hotter, Fatimah's voice echoed behind Khadijah and she heard the words…and on the 7th day he rested." Backing the Benz out of it's parking space and heading toward the highway, Khadijah watched the rear view mirror as the studio went up in flames.

CHAPTER 29

Once I-10 merged into I-20, Khadijah hit cruise control and turned the Benz's satellite radio to a classical Jaz station while programming in a familiar number on the hands-free phone. The straight drive to Atlanta gave her the time to categorize her emotions, a long list, ranging from anger to melancholy and from self-deprecation to understanding. Despite the overall loose tugging at her heart, she couldn't seem to debrief her mind's eye from the disheartening and mind blowing act that her sister had just committed. Be as it may, she also identified with Fatimah's dilemma. Even as kids, Fatimah was her identical opposite, whereas Khadijah was always the bottled up source of good-natured energy, there, lurking in the shadow just beneath the surface, a brooding evil was awaiting to explode and self destruction pushed forward from her sister's personality. One good had just enough weight to balance out the bad". So much time had passed between the sisters , and even though the reunion was healing, the emotional attachment stayed neutral. Watching her twins unfiltered and subhuman suicide, it clipped the umbilical chord of familiarity. Alike in every physical way, their opposing mentalities is what classified them as *identical strangers.*

Thankful that Malik's wisdom took root in her fertile spiritual ground, it was he that realized Khadijah Jenee' Dupree was in fact bottled up inside of herself. Pressing number one on speed dial, she waited for the smooth raspy voice that had become her reflection of reason. "As-alaamu Aleikum." Hearing the simple and unpretentious greeting clouded her eyes with tears. Choking back the bile of rising road rage, Khadijah kept her desires short and sweet. "I need you—not now, but right now! Take all the time you need, but call me when your plane arrives at Hartsfield International." Catching the hurt in her voice, Malik was already mentally preparing for the first class flight to the dirty. Crossing under the 285 overpass, Khadijah could see the airport's runway from the exit and sighed the relief of her nearness to the Radison Hotel just one exit over. Charging the Presidential Suite on her prepaid Rush Card that she used only for emergencies and key card in hand, she made her way hastily to the elevators in a hurry to pamper herself past her pain. Before getting to the room, she realized that Atlanta was not Augusta, and she needed something to wear. Prolonging the attacking of her agony, Khadijah needed to enhance her image, and Greenbrier Mall had to serve as her physical pharmaceutical.

After finding the perfect outfit, Khadijah wandered into the opulent Brazilian beauty salon and treated herself to the house specialty package. Relishing in the final result of the pedicure and manicure, she was finally able to go relax in her room. On the drive back to the Radisson Hotel, Khadijah was reluctant to accept the revelation. While previously in Malik's presence, she always let the pull of attraction and actually thought she sensed the formation of love in the form of a noun. But tonight she needed the action form of the verb. She couldn't wait for the spiritual awakening that manifested itself during every meeting, but she was preparing for the side show, cause she was wounded and needed a little Marvin Gaye in her life.

CHAPTER 30

The vapor rising from the flames formed a tiara around Fatimah's head, crowning her the princess of the underworld. For the first time, her sister seemed happy. Her voice was distorted as if she were under water. Her hands, in the form of burning flesh reached out towards her, so close but yet so far. As if afraid to say Khadijah's name, Fatimah called out and began to talk. "Khadijah, these flames represent what's real. Our characters have always contradicted each other in a complementary sort of way; if we symbolized a coin, you're heads and I'm tails. I embezzled flames from Hell so that you could embrace the fantasies of Heaven. I know you don't understand, but I was your liability. As long as I existed in the physical form, loyalty would have handicapped you from ever having happiness. Allegiance extends beyond the grave. Everybody makes their own decisions in life; there are many facets of ourselves. There exists a killer in us all; there was one in Destiny. Just as Destiny killed, it was her destiny to be killed; death is only an extension of life. Our circumstances held us captive, Khadijah, and my death was the key to unbind your shackles. Not only the restraint of your hands or your feet, but also the cuffs that captured your conscience. Does it make sense to apply for credit when all your debts are paid?"

As her sister backed deeper into the Styx, fading into the fire, Khadijah kicked and clawed her way out of the covers. Pouring perspiration, she awoke out of a cold sweat. Unconscious of her surroundings, she looked around the dark room tempting to focus in on Fatimah's features. Saddened by her dream's sagacity, Khadijah began to wipe away the rivulets of sweat trickling down her body. Snatching the covers back, she shot her hand out in search of her cell phone. Remembrance of Malik's message caused a slight panic. Listening to the voicemail left only seconds ago, she called the front desk and reserved a chauffeur to pick up a Mr. Malik A. Rafsanjani at the airport and deliver him to the hotel. Networking sure made life simple; the hotel had a limousine service on sight at one of the busiest airports in the world. Hopping into the jacuzzi, the heated jet spray began to ease the tension. The warmth melted, layer by layer, shame and guilt over the inner turmoil of her other half. Refreshed and rejuvenated, Khadijah applied just a hint of clear gloss to her lips. While fingering the dog tags around her neck, as if that would help erase that tragic moment in time, she looked herself over in the mirror one final time. Dressed in an Emilio Pucci Flower Print silk caftan, the soft fabric rounding her every curve; she slipped into a matching pair of sunflower yellow Versace zip-up opened toe heels. Smoothing out all the imaginary wrinkles, a knock at the door stole her attention and she calmed her nerves as she walked to the door. Fumbling with the locks like a high school girl going on her senior prom, Khadijah opened the door and fell into Malik's arms. All that cool, calm, and collective shit ran right past them into the hallway. Crying into his shoulder, she managed to recite Surah 60:1 through her sobs. "Don't befriend unbelievers." Pushing her back, holding her by the shoulders at arms length, he saw her beauty cracking through the chaos of mysterious tragedy. Grabbing her chin, Malik kissed her, soaking up her stress like a sponge as they backed into the room and closed the door.

With protective concern oozing from Malik's eyes, Khadijah told him about Fatimah's suicide. Side-stepping his sympathy, the spiritual demons propelled from her pores as she cleansed herself through verbal exorcism. Unable to withstand his recriminating gaze, Khadijah took the cowards way out. Turning around, she allowed the infrared of Malik's mechanical stare to bounce off of her back. If Khadijah had eyes in the back of her head, the constant shift of facial expressions would have definitely impeded on her ability to continue. Emotions from anger to amazement and from altruism to admiration played over the surface of Malik's features. She peeked occasionally to discern the damage to the relationship she was doing. Squeezing her taut shoulders, he massaged away enough of the tension to make Khadijah comfortable in her confession.

At this point, touch moved mountains; the simple gesture held a complex meaning. It signified, "I'm here and I'm yours." With the confidence returning, Khadijah turned to face her fears. Grabbing his hands, she explained, "It's hard to watch someone whose being, and beginning, is the same as yours, commit suicide." It was in that instant when the flames fanned out around her, and she willfully tackled death. It's the duplicity of negative and positive weight that keeps us calibrated. If she could so humbly accept the most incorrigible death possible, then I can at least honor her heroism with a complimentary last ditch leap at life. Sharing myself with you puts me on even keel, there exists no over-exaggerated loves, and all of my outstanding hate has been finally laid to rest. Halting her with his hands, Malik guided Khadijah's head to his shoulders. Enjoying the silky touch of her hair, he said to her, "Although, it's the DeoxyriboNucleic Acid in the blood running through your veins that makes you who you are, it's the people who love you that makes you what you are."

"The problem is that you lived without love for too long. I just hope that you are conducive to change. Now, it's time to fill the vacuum of your future so that you may excel instead of merely exist. Matter, scientifically, can be neither created nor destroyed, and your soul is the matter that God give purpose." Taking Malik's hands, she responded, "If actions are absolute, that makes Fatimah's affinity unconditional. That's my only example of what love may be. Her death will always plague me, but I've enshrined my sister in the memorial of my mind." In her vulnerability, gone was the masked image she put on for the world.

CHAPTER 31

The overhead sign read: Welcome to Augusta, as Khadijah veered off of the Washington Rd. exit, wanting to be in familiar territory as she and Malik embarked on new encounters that would solidify their relationship. Taking a few stolen moments to allow Malik to process all of her revelations on the two hour drive from the ATL, Khadijah told him her feelings of her studies of Islam in his absence. As the bright lights of Augusta's busiest street came flooding into the interior of the Benz, Khadijah held a beautiful and mysterious smile on her face telling him, "Welcome to my world." Getting to the sour side of the conversation, she began to explain her fears and reservations concerning religion.

"I think Islam is a beautiful way of life but I'm not attracted to the reduction of women displayed by the doctrine. Malik, I refuse to go from the embers of my own personal Hell here on Earth to being punished pursuant to the flames of your, or any man's, demands and emotions." Seeing the shock registered in his eyes, Khadijah recited a Surah from the Qu'ran that she seemed to take offense to. Surah An-Nisa 4:34:

The men have authority over the woman due to the excellence which Allah has given to the man over the woman,

and due to the wealth that they spend upon them.

Maybe in my ignorance, I have misconstrued the meaning, but the passage creates the vision of chattel slavery. I'm too independent to be reduced to a slave again. As a people, we've been there and done that; I can't see willfully regressing to a religious plantation. Don't get me wrong, I don't mind being submissive to my man, but submission doesn't equate to the position of being someone's property. Trust me, I am willing to learn and absorb the ways and workings of the faith, because I understand that there's expectations and guidelines as a Muslim that we must all adhere to. Any man who possesses the insight, wisdom, and patience that it took to open me up, spiritually, has my devotion. Even though I didn't behave like it, I always believed in God. My memories of my mother are angelic in their own way. Out of ignorance, my understanding is still in the innocent stage of an infant, and I would hate to be ostracized, denied, and reduced to ignobility because of being spiritually illiterate. I've been studying because I'm lost, and the search is the byproduct of suffering. Malik, the strongest impetus a woman will ever have is a man she admires. In an individual sense, you are that impetus for me, and I'm dependent on your leadership. I look to your strength and direction; subconsciously you've become my rock and my pillar of stability."

Turning into the oyster bar, Khadijah told Malik to wait in the car and she would be right back. Watching the slow and fluid motion of her hips, he could feel his excitement shift in his lap. Thankful for a few minutes of solitude, Malik searched his mind. He had to help this woman find clarity out of clutter. The silence was broken and Khadijah drove across the four lane and parked the car in Fat Tuesday's parking lot. Carrying the bushel of oysters, Malik followed Khadijah to a patio table where they had all the privacy they needed. The waitress took their drink orders and they asked for a set of paper plates and napkins. The atmosphere was relaxing. While waiting for their drinks to arrive, Malik began explaining that he understood her reservations regarding the Islamic religion and said that the more she grew, the more she would comprehend. Malik shared a sermon by the Honorable Minister Louis Farrakhan, "People are like pegs, their roots are hidden. Take, for example, a mountain… if it's a mile high, the root has to be a mile deep. The heights and depths are equal!" Fatimah understood this concept more than anyone. She ultimately served as the post of plurality. She realized that as long as she stayed attached, her depth would only cancel out Khadijah's heights; one's human, moral, and spiritual elevation would never depart from ground level. "Biblically, God created us in his likeness. In Islam, this is referred to as Khalifa. It simply means one who stands in the place of another or one who succeeds another." Interrupting their conversation, the waitress sat their drinks and plates at the table. Pulling the bushel of raw oysters out of the bag, Malik placed some on his and her plates. Teasing him a little, she popped open the shell and slowly sucked the oyster out. Smiling from the insinuation, Malik licked his oyster out of the shell while raising the tip of his tongue and staring into Khadijah's beautiful brown eyes. Both sipping their alcoholic slushes, inebriation started to settle and the aphrodisiac started taking its course. "Malik, you're young, intelligent, and successful, not to mention that your intelligence is attractive. I'm horny and I want you in the same way that I've had to endure life… fast, hard, and rough!" Leaving a tip, they packed up in a hurry.

Taking Broad Street until they reached San Bar Ferry Road, Khadijah turned left into the Old Town section of the city. True to its name, there were very big, old houses that had to have been constructed in the early 1900's. Every house had pillars that lead to the porch. Parking in the driveway, Khadijah was so turned on and excited that as soon as Malik entered into the restored baby mansion, they were tearing at each others clothes. The built up anticipation had become unattainable. Naked and not ashamed, they stumbled their way to the first bedroom they found. Laying Malik down and straddling on top of him, Khadijah was leaking pools at a time of her juices across his abdomen.

Taking his fingers and sucking on them one by one… his thumb, his index finger, his middle finger, and so on; taking his other hand, Khadijah did the same thing. Kissing down his body, she reached his hardness, tracing the outline of her lips with the thick head. Just like with Malik's fingers, she sucked him between her warm, wet lips. Even slower this time, she took his manhood deep, letting her tongue graze his balls before reversing the motion. As his shift slid against the roof of her mouth, Khadijah snaked her tongue over the huge vein on the underside of his dick. Wrapping her long silky black hair around his hand, Malik's toes curled as she repeatedly sucked up and down his hard flesh. Picking up her pace, she brought him to the brink of orgasm a few more times, but wouldn't let him cum just yet.

CHAPTER 32

After the foreplay, Khadijah crawled back on top and looked in to his eyes. Grabbing all eight inches and placing just the swollen head inside of her tight opening, Khadijah whispered, "Tonight we create, so let the construction begin!" Forcing herself to open up to him, her juices started flowing freely. The energy of friction caused a glow around them as Khadijah placed her hands on Malik's chest and wound her hips and took him to the land of milk and honey. Smacking and squeezing her ass, they began sweating profusely. Leaning over like a jockey on the last leg of the Triple Crown, she was working her muscles up and down his pole. Growling and grunting, Khadijah switched directions during the apex of animal lust; easing off of him, she placed her back to him and eased him back inside of her womb. Reaching over and grabbing his ankles for leverage, her back involuntarily arched, and her ass spread wide like the span of an angel's wings. Forcefully smacking her deep chocolate cheeks activated Khadijah's thug nature. Rolling her hips while bouncing up and down on Malik's dick, she screamed and moaned, and he grew longer, harder, and stroked her deeper. The sex sounds and smells their bodies produced released Viagra like properties inside of Malik's system.

Spreading that ass wider, he aggressively pulled her down on the dick to take the excess skin that eased through the feverishly moist intersection of Khadijah's insides. "Ooh yes, Malik, feed me more of tha magic stick."

The smacking of his hands on ass caused Khadijah's pussy to make that wet gushing sound as if he were feeding her dick through a straw. Leaning up and propping on his elbows, Malik was amazed at how her body went from thin flowing juices that ran from the head of his dick and down his thighs to pool in the sheets, to coming out in thick globs of intense heat. Not able to watch the nature of their love making and contain the pure God-given pleasure that Khadijah was giving, he came deep inside of her essence as he half moaned, part growled, and screamed out his love for her.

There's something magical about the word love itself, because with its escape from his lips, Khadijah's valves opened up as she started to tremble and constrict around his manhood. Her release was the energy force that caused her to collapse and shake as if having a seizure.

Laying now with her back flat against his chest, panting as their bodies fought for oxygen, Malik still felt light tremors coursing through her body as the orgasms continued to attack. Involuntarily, her hips danced to their own tune as her vaginal secretions constantly soultrained through her thighs and landed in the sheets. Kissing her neck, Malik whispered how he'd thought about nothing except her since that night in San Diego. Turning over to lay chest to chest and look into his eyes, she made her intentions clear. This time when they departed, it would be in opposite directions for good or the same direction forever. "Malik, sex to me has never been for pleasure until now; it's been more so a tool or device, used when necessary to capture my prey and kill 'em. I gave you all that I know how, in every way that I know how tonight, because it was in your presence that I was introduced to possibilities that no other human being has given to me. Emotions and feelings materialized, and I don't intend to hold you hostage to a situation in which you don't want to be held."

"You, Khadijah Dupree, in fact it was you who helped to define her. The bad, ugly, and the good that you saw and extracted is what I have to offer. What you see and what you make, ultimately, is what you get!" Rubbing his hands lightly up and down the vertebrae of her spine, he cradled the back of Khadijah's neck in his hands and brought her lips down to meet his—lips and tongue shattering the protective coating of souls. Malik eased her off of him and carried her to the shower. Placing her to her feet, he pulled her to him and brushed her lips and said, "Let's enjoy the feelings of satiation in silence, we'll talk when we finish. Let's take a shower together." As the steam rose around their bodies and they embraced, every nerve ending was raw as their energy was exchanged.

As Khadijah's brain and insecurities worked overtime; she felt the chemical compounds of love tugging at her heart, this only served to widen the gap of her soul. Finally, her spirit has met its mate.

CHAPTER 33

A knock at the door startled Jaz out of her dream. Putting on her robe, Ms. Winters asked herself why she couldn't get the twins out of her system. Over eighteen years and she still held this maternal need to protect them. Maybe it was because she failed to shelter the girls when they really needed her the most. Or, could the obsession be something altogether different? With all of her success and accolades, there was no one to inherit the fruits of her labor, and the biological clock was fresh out of batteries. Out of guilt and secrecy, only two graves held the remains of her covert affection and affinity for Khadijah and Fatimah Dupree.

Glancing through the peephole in the door, she noticed the black windbreakers with the yellow lettering stenciled across the chest. "Who's there?" "Ms. Jazmine

Winter, this is the F.B.I., and we need to speak to you about someone that you have worked closely with over the years." Requesting to see their identification, Jazmine studied their credentials closely and asked for a few moments to put on some clothing. Opening the door, the agents introduced themselves and advised her that they were with the Louisiana Homicide and Terrorism Division. Sensing her defensive nature, they assured her there was no need to panic. "We found the dental remains of a Mrs. Gloria Klein in the ash and rubble of a burned down studio in Lake Charles, Louisiana. There we also two identified males and one other Jane Doe" We don't have a motive or theory for this tragedy, but we did notice after going through Mrs. Klein's case files, that the two men were tied up in the Dupree Case that you two worked together. After studying the files for this particular case, we have uncovered corruption on Mrs. Klein's behalf. It appears as if she were bribed to push the credentials and paperwork for retired military officers Sexton and Rosecrans through. Notes also reveal that as the child psychologist on this case, that you were dead set agains the adoption. Can you tell us a little about your strong opposition to the outcome of that case?'"Well agents, that case was a very long time ago, and of course I was opposed to the girls being separated for the sake of closing the file. My opinion was strong then and I'll go to my grave standing behind the final summation of the case. What all this has to do with the tragedy is beyond me, but I'm smart enough to know that the Federal Bureau of Investigations has a theory of its own. As for a Mr. Sexton and Mr. Rosecrans, I met them once, for all of thirty minutes. That's about how long it took me to plead my case for the welfare of those precious little girls." "Ms. Winters, there are too many vacancies in the case and even though we know that Mrs. Klein was paid a king's ransom to prequalify these men for adoption, the highway of financial records has been closed down. A foundation has been laid; along with the facts that all three players are dead, we have no leads or motives! This was our last ditch effort to solve this mystery. That's life, we win some, and we lose some! I have the point of ignition, and it appears that our Jane Doe killed everybody, including herself. Thank you for your time. If it's possible, can we get your signature on this voluntary information sheet? This case is now closed, sealed, and concluded as a homicide/suicide. Thank you for your time Ms. Winters."

With the echo of the closing door, Jaz, as Khadijah

and Fatimah affectionately referred to her, couldn't hold back the onslaught of tears. Now she knew the reasons for her dreams as of late. Figuring that she would never see the girls again after they met down on Mission Beach, she could also close this chapter of the Duprees forever. Jazmine cried alligator tears for both Fatimah and Khadijah. She studied their strengths and weaknesses and knew that no matter how cruel and mean little Khadijah could be when it came to her sister, that it was Fatimah who had no conscience. Whatever they found in their mother's annals set them off. They must have somehow figured out Mrs. Klein's involvement. Wanting to search deeper to find out just how deep this hole had been dug, she called Charlie Puetz, who'd been their lawyer for so long.

After changing pleasantries, she explained to him her visit from the F.B.I., and although the girls were never mentioned, she gave him her theory as well. "Jazmine, from my lips to your ears, this cover up was way deeper than child Protection Services.It's a military conspiracy that happens all the time and gets lost in the shuffle! The government has laws of its own, and the feds showing up at your doorstep proves it. They know more than they're letting on; they just wanted to see how much you really knew. I know you are confused, but they just covered up a cover up. One that could expose Uncle Sam and the U.S. Military." Damn, she couldn't believe all of this murder and devastation to protect a few "Chicks with Dicks," all in the name of Don't ask, don't tell. To hell with military policy! Everybody thought her brother was crazy. Uncle Sam had dismantled his character, thereby crashing his credibility. She was glad that she possessed every letter with dates, times, and names, but damn, Jaz, what's your next move?

CHAPTER 34

The brisk leaves rustled throughout the Arlington National Cemetery as Khadijah and Malik made their way to Destiny's grave marker. With more purpose in her step than any other previous visit, Khadijah pulled Malik along as she half skipped and half ran to reveal her peace and inner joy to the site that contained her mother's energy. Almost as if she was having an out-of-body experience, her hate began to dissolve, and she could now feel all the pride that servicemen must enjoy, day in and day out, while their lives are being placed on the line. Single tears formed in the corner of each eye while she offered her man over to her mother. "Destiny, this is Malik, your soon to be son-in-law." Pulling his arms around her tightly, "He's my Muslim Marvin Sapp!"

"Hello Ms. Dupree, I've heard so much about you and I'm proud, as well as honored, to add your legacy to my life. So many failed to protect you, but you still leave an imprint on history that no pencil can erase. "You are, and forever will be, a heroine in my eyes, and I'm elated to keep your story and dreams alive. You've lost one daughter to the struggle, but she gave herself up so freely, just so that Khadijah could break the cycle of hate that Kaifeng, after death, had produced for your girls. Fatimah made the ultimate sacrifice for her twin, and even in their lust for revenge, it was love that conquered all! As I ask you for Khadijah's hand in marriage; I hope the octave of my heart carries to your ears in paradise. I know you are smiling down on your daughter. She bent, but wasn't broken by the circumstances that caused her heart to harden. Destiny I'm leaving this vase of sunflowers because they represent you. Even as the flower dies away, it's seeds will scatter the ground and constantly reproduce. Allah/God is the greatest of all planners, and these moments were already written. Just as you have, Khadijah and I will continue to fulfill our purpose."

Stepping away, Malik stood off at a distance and gave Khadijah the space to talk privately with her mother. Watching her on her knees, it pained Malik to see his wife-to-be release all the stored up hurt as she shared secrets untold with her mother. He knew his presence gave her the strength to purge herself and break free from her demons, "Sometimes doing nothing and saying less is all the support one needs." After all the words had ceased and the silence set in, Khadijah just stared into the sky. Malik lifted her up from behind and got down on one knee. Producing the black velvet box from the pocket of his mid-length leather bomber, he took her hand and said, "When we leave here today, we step into a new beginning. All debts have been paid!" Slipping the ring on her finger, he asked, "Will you marry me? Be careful what you say, your mom is our witness." Both laughing and crying, she pulled him up and they departed from the cemetery, ready to start all over.

On the drive back to Augusta, Khadijah convinced Malik that she needed to make one more trip to San Diego to get her mother's things and visit her child psychologist Jazmine Winters. Confused by the request, Khadijah explained that there were a few issues she still needed to work though and the only person she trusted was her childhood psych, Ms. Winters. Seeing the immediate questions swirling around in Malik's head, she grabbed his hand and assured him that chapter of her life was officially closed. Making a joke of the situation, she teased him that since he gave her the magic stick, all she ever wanted to do was create life, not end it! Besides, she needed one final counseling session because there was something eating at her. Jaz resembled, too closely, the man in her mother's pictures; the resemblance was too strong to be just another coincidence. Pulling the cellphone from his pocket to make the reservations, Khadijah stopped him; she wanted to drive. There was a roadside marker dedicated to her mother at the site where the accident had claimed her life, that she had yet to see.

The last leg of the three thousand mile trip from Augusta to California was wound through the dangerous and often-times fatal Yuma, Arizona mountains. Behind the wheel, Malik was amazed at the up and down mountainside drive. Luckily traffic was light at the break of dawn. Gasping for her breath, Khadijah choked as she saw it for the first time. The sign read, Destiny Dupree's Corner; Be aware of the steep decline to 1600 ft below sea level, and please watch for trucks. Deep in thought, their ears popped and the air seemed thicker as they finally saw the bright lights of the weigh station and checkpoint entering into California. Traffic slowed to a crawl as patrol walked around with drug dogs while searching for unpermitted fruits being smuggled into the area.

CHAPTER 35

Walking into the office of Jazmine Winters, the receptionist asked if Malik and Khadijah had an appointment. They advised her that they didn't but really needed to see Dr. Winters; and after giving their names, they were sure that she would indeed fit them in. Aggravated by their persistence, the secretary picked up the phone advising her boss that there was a Khadijah Dupree along with an Mr. Malik Rafsanjani in the office lobby to see her. Jaz advised her to tell them that she would be through with her client in about fifteen minutes and to seat them in her huge conference room. She would join them shortly.

Flipping through the latest issues of *Essence* and *Ebony* magazines, a smile sprouted as Jaz burst through the door, as if the building were on fire. Running into the arms of the only mother she ever knew, the flood gate of tears opened and Malik sat and took in their exchange. Instant admiration flaring for Ms. Winters, he stood to introduce himself to this woman that obviously had an impact on Khadijah. As the two women broke their embrace, Jazmine automatically noticed the three carat pear shaped diamond engagement ring. Smiling at the stunned expression, Khadijah said, "Let me introduce you to my king. This is my fiance' and soon-to-be husband, Malik Rafsanjani; and this Malik, is Jazmine Winters—world renowned psychologist and the only mother figure me or my late sister has ever known." Stiffening at the word 'late', Jaz knew that her intuition was dead on, however, there was a time and place for everything. Grabbing Khadijah's hand, she motioned at the ring; Jaz said, "It's obvious the biggest surprises come in the smallest packages." Advising Malik to make himself comfortable while they went to her office for a little girl's talk, Khadijah and Jaz disappeared to share life changing gossip between them.

Listening intently, Jaz couldn't contain her sorrow at the revelation of Fatimah's untimely demise. Assuming is one thing … but, hearing was another sort of pain altogether. With her jaw hanging damned near flush on the desk at the lives the girls had led due to the harsh injustices of the faulty Child Protective Service Agencies and good ole Uncle Sam, Jazmine was formulating a plan to expose the hidden corruption that existed in both government agencies. Now, it was time for Jaz to reveal a shocking secret of her own! Destiny and Jazmine were closer than sisters, in fact, Destiny was engaged to her brother, the late Seaman Bush. He was, in fact, her twin! Khadijah knew she saw a resemblance and now, pulling the picture from her pocket, looking from Jaz to the picture, they were also identical. Not wanting to talk about Malik behind his back, Khadijah suggested his return.

Entering the arena of shared secrets, Khadijah told him she'd shared all details with Jazmine, except for what she now had to say, "Jaz, this is the man that saved me from myself. He jump-started my ability to facilitate change. Also, he broke down, brick-by-brick, the mental and emotional prison that I had confined myself to. Malik aided and abetted me in what I like to call the great mental escape. He's been at my every beckoned call since our introduction. A little history, he's Muslim, born and raised in Chicago, and owns his own accounting firm.""Wow, it's a small world! I never knew I would meet my homeboy this way." Stunned, both Khadijah and Malik's head whipped around to stare at Jazmine. Yes, I'm also a Chi-Raq export, raised on 91st and Emerald right off Halsted Street. In fact, I was just there a few weeks ago. You know us city girls…. had to whip these butters Chi-Town style!" She patted her hair as Khadijah picked up on the Mid-West slang. "I had to stock up on my old school house music, and you know, I had to have me some of that Harold's Chicken." She high-fived Malik as they basked in the glow of shared cultural experience.

"Getting back to the story, my brother brought me out here when he got stationed in San Diego, took me on as his dependent, and made Uncle Sam send me to San Diego State." "Khadijah, when they sent my brother to prison, your mom wanted to marry him any way. She believed in him and trusted him. They were best friends and he wouldn't marry Destiny, because he knew that Uncle Sam would try to use that against her, to disqualify her from some of the things he was coaching her to accomplish. My brother was a fighter and he died fighting for the rights of your mother to be preserved. He set the bar real high for your mom. She never stopped loving him. They made a hell of a team and went to bat for each other. When men in the military told her she could not achieve this, or a woman is not allowed to do that, he fought the powers that be to give her a chance. Once he got the door opened, he would physically, and mentally train Destiny for the psychological and extremely strenuous physical regimen that they were sure to put her through. Even from behind bars, he was able to coach her through the traps and pitfalls that they had put into place, to ensure her failure! At one point, I even advised Destiny to say 'the hell with Uncle Sam', because they would eventually kill her. She would always respond … 'Or make me stronger.'"

When he found out about the six man black operation, they were assigned to in Somalia, Bush made Destiny grow her hair real long and showed her how to tie it in a boatswains knot, to make it look like a bun. Our grandfather was a blacksmith and taught my brother how to make knives with precision. He sent her to find the particular steel that she needed from one of our grandfather's friends at Central Pacific Railroad and coached her to craft the tool that would eventually save her life. It was a lightweight dagger that fit precisely in the bun of her hair, and she trained with it there for weeks.

"Now you know why I always spent so much time with you and Fatimah; also, that's why I took your case in the first place. After they killed my brother, Destiny was all the family I had left, and besides me, you twins was all she had. Now it looks like we all we got! I have some letters that my brother wrote to me before he died explaining everything the military was trying to do and the reasons for their actions that I want you to have a copy of. I'm going to expose them for what they took from us. Not quite sure how, just yet, but it will happen. Before you leave, I need you to fill out some papers. You are my beneficiary and if anything happens to me, then I want you to have it all. When your mother was raped and my brother realized she was pregnant, it was he who came up with your names. To your mom and my brother, you were flesh of his flesh. Sorry you never got the chance to meet him, but he loved you and Fatimah when all that existed was a clot. Khadijah, make no mistake, when the government gets wind of what I'm up to, they will kill me! Malik, this is where you come in. I need you and Khadijah to reproduce as many of us as possible. Make sure I get my invitation hot off the press."

"Jazmine, being one of my fellow Chicagoans, you were birthed under one of, if not the most, corrupt governments that exist. I know that out of anger you want to retaliate, hell so do I—for my own personal reasons, but it's the cycle of revenge that has us here today. Khadijah, I and children all over the world need you. Since the recording of the history of the U.S. government, there's been one cover up after another. They are the masters of their own game. You don't need revenge because you hold the power. If you didn't, do you think any of us would still be alive? They expect you to come forward with this knowledge so they can track and finally destroy the evidence. Once you make it public, that's exactly what will happen. Do you think Uncle Sam likes turning his head in the other direction while members of his fraternal order lose their lives? Hell no, but shame and the continuity of concealing government faults has allocated servicemen to become casualties of war. So far, silence has been the deadliest weapon you possess, but soon as you make this information public, you will definitely loose the war! You have fought enough, and you have also survived. The hard lessons of slavery was to play ignorant to the Master's ploys and plots. The only way to understand the oppressor's language was to learn to read and write. Learning to intellectualize on their level, while walking in the shadows of ignorance were the biggest weapons that the slaves had. True enough, you could go forth with this information and shock the world for a day, but before the investigation even starts, all traces of you and the evidence you hold will be washed away at sea. Take our Honorable minister, Louis Farrakhan for example, as long as he was publicizing his intentions and revealing all that he was aware of, the government went to great lengths to silence him. From cutting off finances to attempting to tarnish Muslim credibility on a global scale. When you overexpose your hand, you are no longer a threat. Now, your felicity comes every time you look into the eyes of the antagonists and pass that shared secret energy that they were not able to oppress, Jaz, that's power!"

"Now, as far as your invitation being hot off the press, in Islam, marriage is a union created through contract. However, we will put together something to commemorate our union. Besides, there are some very important people that I would like to introduce you to. I think our sweetest revenge will come in the form of legislation. Malcolm X said it best, 'Power is not in the bullet, but in the ballot!'"

CHAPTER 36

Back at the beach house, a cool breeze blew through the open windows while Jaz, Khadijah, and Malik sat around going through Destiny's treasured journals as they gave meaning and credence to her short-lived life. Malik recognized a picture of Bush, right from the start. Keeping secrets of his own, he still remembered the talk they had when he was homeless and trying to find his way. It was Bush who took him to the Mosque on 79th, and his departing words were, "Lil man, this is the best life I know to give you. These cold streets of Chicago done sucked so much of my soul that I got to find my way out. Introducing you to some of my Muslim friends is far better than seeing you sucked up by these streets. A man is only as good as his purpose in life, and I would hate to see you never define yours.

Every day I passed you wandering aimlessly in these streets, I searched my heart for ways I could help. By bringing you to Islam, I know there will be both structure and curriculum instilled to created and facilitate purpose and progress in life, where at the present there is none. While you go in one direction to make some sense out of your life, I'll be going in another direction trying to do the same with mine. If I'm ever in these parts again, I will make it my business to find you Lil Man, but my plan is to leave and never look back." Minister Shareef Ali had snapped a picture of them outside the temple gates and it's one that he had kept over the years. Malik's abnormal gaze at the picture raised questions in Jaz and Khadijah's minds. Seeing the moisture accumulate around the whites of his eyes, Malik reached for his wallet and pulled out the wallet-sized photo of him and Bush standing outside of the Muslim mosque.

Amazed at how diminutive the world really was, the three kicked off their shoes and headed for the solace of Mission Beach. Strolling along the sandy shore, water coursed through their feet as Malik recounted his experience of Jazmin's brother. Life, in itself, interconnects everything and everyone, if they dig deep enough.

Packing as much as their car could hold, Khadijah and Jazmin Winters hugged and said their good-byes while Malik waited behind the wheel for another cross-country trip. Humbled by this encounter, Khadijah and Malik used every mile as a marker to process and internalize all of the information they had been introduce to. With quietness came clarity. The two of them seemed to appreciate the tranquility of the long drive. With still so many unsolved issues standing between them, there would be a lot of preparation and planning in the days to come. Marriage was a big step, but Khadijah was willing to compromise and sacrifice. Pulling into the driveway of the massive home, Malik cut the engine, kissed his fiancé and said, "Finally, we're home." Not catching the intended meaning, Khadijah went about the routine of unloading the car. When they were finished unpacking, Destiny had a room of her own. In a few days, Malik and Khadijah would create a real memorial dedicated to the life, death, and legacy of Destiny Dupree.

CHAPTER 37

Nervous and sort of uneasy, Jazmine Winters waited with quiet confidence while the Joint Chief of Staff and the Secretary of State reviewed the letters and years of compiled evidence that deceased Seaman Bush had put together.

Clearly agitated with the woman's insinuations and accusations of homosexuality and cover-ups by some of the great men in uniform, to create a deep-rooted conspiracy theory, they had to find another approach to a problem, that if gone public, would surely unveil an embarrassing scandal on behalf of the U.S. Military. "Ms. Winters, there has obviously been a gross miscarriage of justice concerning the deceased. I'm hoping we can come up with a swift resolution that will put all of this behind us, without embarrassing our country. Nothing can be done to reverse the loss of lives, however, I believe we can resolve this situation amicably." Not wanting to trust in their show of good faith, Jazmine insisted that she record the rest of this meeting, as well as that the conditions be put into writing, on official U.S. Military stationary. Rushing to retrieve the stenographer, the JAG lawyers set up the machine, and as soon as everybody had taken their places began to read off the conditions in which they had been ordered to adhere to and abide by:

1) The military records be made to reflect my brother's honorable tenure of service

2) A new DD214 revised

3) That the trumped-up court martial and conviction, at the least, be fully pardoned and all blemishes erased from the service record

4) His insurance policy honored and paid to the rightful beneficiary

5) That full internal investigation be done on the operation in Africa in which officers Sexton and Rosecrans turned their backs while seaman Destiny Dupree was captured, raped, sodomized, and tortured

CHAPTER 38

It was a glorious summer day in Augusta, Georgia. The crowded pavilion was a melting pot of religious beliefs as Christians, Muslims, Catholics, and persons of non-denominational ties all gathered for the uniting ceremony of Mr. Malik A. Rafsanjani and Mrs . Khadijah Dupree Rafsanjani. The beaming bride sucked the air out of those in attendance as she marched up the aisles, adorned in her silk and satin thobe with a matching lace hijab, to cover her head, as well as the niqab that concealed the pronounced features of her beautiful face. Standing at the alter in all her glory, her heart dropped as Malik and two of his brothers from the mosque, each released a pure white dove into the atmosphere. The first symbolized the past, which brought them together. The second was a reminder of the present in which to look back would take them off

the course of their divine destiny, and the third represent-
ing the wings of their future as husband and wife.

ACKNOWLEDGEMENTS

First and foremost, I would like to acknowledge God as the Creator and Sustainer of my life. With that said, I want to give a very special thanks to my beautiful wife Kisha Lawton for always challenging and driving me to be better. Blondell L. Weaver, without you there is no me. Margot Weaver Hale and Yolanda Marie Bush you are the Angel's that sit to the left and the right of me.

To my mentor and literary counselor Juva Threat Alexander, thank you for being a constant voice and a wealth of information in my state of ignorance on this journey. Lisa T. William's, you are an invaluable asset to my overall success and even when life knocks us down, just know the power lies in getting back up!

To those who held me down and became my reasons to push hard through my period of incarceration, thanks for your love, loyalty and dedication. Your never giving up on me is what gave me the strength to not give up on myself. Natashia Bush Hills, Esq. and Lovenia B. Mathews, you were the prescription in my time of sickness!

Ms. Arilia Winn and Winn Publications, words are not enough. You gave me the opportunity to make this dream a reality. You and the staff at Winn Publications are the bomb, thanks for allowing me to express the creative side of me that up until this point most never even knew existed.

To the late, great Cleveland Bush, Jr., my heart still hurts from losing you. You were not only a father, you were a friend. In a world where Black boys grew up in homes without the guidance of a father, you stayed ten toes down and fought the trials and tribulations toe-to-toe with me. When you gained your wings, you flew a part of me to Heaven.

Last but not least, Ashante' and Allante' Harrison, you are my first infatuation with the nature of twins. That infatuation has manifested in this work and I want to thank you all for inspiring me to create.

CLEVELAND BUSH III BIOGRAPHY

Cleveland Bush III, born November 20, 1973 in a sub-urban town of Chicago, Illinois called Robbins. He is the son of Blondell Weaver and the late Cleveland Bush Jr. He has two siblings. Grew up in Chicago and North Augusta, South Carolina. Permanently relocating to South Carolina in 1990, Cleveland graduated from North Augusta High School in 1992. He is a Veteran of the United States Navy, and a twenty (20) year survivor of mass incarceration, where he learned the valuable art of survival through faith. He is a powerful and skilled orator, blogger, author, and entrepreneur. Currently residing in Columbia, South Carolina and working as a Winding Technician in the fiberglass industry. Considered to be a loving and devoted husband, awesome brother, and a loyal and honest friend.

Cleveland has educated numerous audiences on crime and punishment, and the familial, as well as personal, effects of incarceration. He's been invited to speak to at-risk youth groups, inmates, high school athletes, mothers raising children in a hostile society, hospice care groups, homeless communities, and other social economic groups.It's his deep passion for turning the amalgamation of life experiences and fantasy into enchanting thrillers to provide excellent reading material for a wide range of audiences.

Humbled by experience, he shares his badge of honor with the greatest men who have walked this earth—Jesus Christ, Martin Luther King Jr., Malcolm X, Nelson Mandela and Mr. Barak Obama.

His accolades include, but are not limited to: High school diploma, Electricity & Electronics Certification (USN), and an Associates, B.S., Masters, and P.H.D., all from the school of hard knocks, by way of various prison mentalities and environments.

www.ingramcontent.com/pod-product-compliance
Lightning Source LLC
Chambersburg PA
CBHW071358100726
47908CB00004B/1030